STAY WITH ME

A LAZARUS RISING STORY

New York Times and USA Today Bestselling Author

CYNTHIA EDEN

This book is a work of fiction. Any similarities to real people, places, or events are not intentional and are purely the result of coincidence. The characters, places, and events in this story are fictional.

Published by Cynthia Eden.

Copyright ©2017 by Cynthia Eden

Proof-reading by: J. R. T. Editing

CHAPTER ONE

"I found you."

Shelly Hampton stilled when she heard those low, rough words. A chill slid over her spine. And then...a heavy, warm hand curled around her shoulder.

Clutching her bag tightly to her chest, Shelly turned to face—well, she had no idea who the man was. She had to look up, way up, to see his features. Shelly barely topped five feet, and this giant of a guy with his broad chest and his linebacker shoulders had to be way over six feet tall.

The man was big, but in a muscled, *I-Workout-All-The-Time* way. His muscles stretched the black t-shirt he wore. *A t-shirt? As cold as it is outside?* His skin was a soft olive, a faint stubble of black covered his hard jaw, and his dark hair was cut almost brutally short. A military cut.

His eyes—the most piercing blue she'd ever seen—were locked on her. Light, *light* blue. The guy actually seemed to be staring at her with a bit of...wonder in his gaze? No, no, couldn't be wonder. That didn't make any sense. Had to be something else.

"I found you," he said again, and his hold tightened on her.

Shelly forced a smile. All around her, she could hear voices rising and falling. She was in a bar on the edge of Discovery, a small speck of a town in the Blue Ridge Mountains. Locals and tourists had crowded into the little bar for some holiday celebration time, but she'd only come inside for a quick pit stop.

The stranger before her was handsome, if you liked the rough, rugged kind of guy. She did. And normally, Shelly would have been all about some flirtation with him, but… "I'm afraid you have me confused with someone else." Shelly tucked a lock of her dark hair behind her ear. "I don't know you."

He blinked. A slow, almost robotic move. "You…don't?"

"No, sorry." She waved vaguely toward the crowd and tried to ignore the fact that his touch was making her stomach knot. "Maybe the woman you're looking for is sitting at one of the tables. There are lots of women with dark hair in here tonight—"

"I'm not looking for lots of women." A muscle flexed in his square jaw. His eyes had narrowed, seeming to turn into chips of blue ice. "I've been looking for you."

Okay. Wait. Perhaps he was trying to use some sort of pick-up line on her? If that was the case, well, he needed to work on his technique. Because the guy was totally coming off a bit stalkerish. And with all of the drama she'd had in her life, that kind of thing was a serious turn-off. "I'm not here to hook-up." Honesty was always supposed to be the best policy. "But I'm sure a guy like you will have no trouble finding plenty of interested partners." She slid away from his hold and made her way toward the wooden bar that stretched along the back of the building. She didn't look back over her shoulder, but Shelly could have sworn that she felt the stranger's eyes on her with every step she took.

Her boots shuffled across the floor until she reached the bar. She leaned over the scarred surface, waving to get the attention of the bartender/owner of the joint. Sammy Wisemore caught her eye and he winked, then he hurried toward her, wiping his hands on the big, white apron that he always wore—an apron that was as white as Sammy's hair. The guy had to be pushing eighty, but he moved with the energy of a man half his age.

"Shelly!" He gave her hand a warm squeeze. "Got the keys for you. Give me just a minute."

She smiled at him and hoped she didn't look nervous. *Don't look over your shoulder.* She was *not* going to peek back at the stranger.

Sammy reached under the bar and a moment later, he was handing her a key ring. "I got the cabin all ready for you yesterday. Stocked with plenty of firewood and food. You'll be good to go."

In addition to owning the bar, Sammy was also the caretaker of her family's cabin. He'd been one of her father's closest friends, and growing up, she'd enjoyed visiting "Uncle" Sammy.

For just a moment, sadness clouded Sammy's eyes. "You sure you want to be alone up there? You know I got that apartment right over the bar. You can stay in town, and I can keep you company."

He was so good to her. Always had been. But this time, being alone was exactly what she wanted. No, it was what she needed. She couldn't stay over the bar — there were far too many people there. "I'll be okay." Now she was the one to give his hand a quick squeeze before she took the keys from him. "Besides, you'll come visit me on Christmas, won't you?"

"Hell, yes, I — "

Sammy's words stopped or at least, she thought they did. She wasn't sure because suddenly, the stranger was there again. Big, strong, and he was touching her shoulder once more. Only his touch was hesitant. So careful.

And she found herself turning away from Sammy. Staring at the man who dominated the whole place.

"You know me." There was a hint of desperation in the stranger's voice.

Shelly licked her lips, and the man's gaze immediately fell to her mouth. "I'm sorry," she told him. "But we don't know each other."

His hand slid to her cheek. "I…remember."

"Get your hand off her, buddy." That was Sammy's voice. He didn't sound like his usual, cheerful self. He sounded pissed and angry.

The stranger's hand fell away. A furrow appeared between his brows.

"Who are you?" Shelly whispered. Because there was just something about him…he looked lost. So alone in that crowd of laughing, happy people.

His thick lashes shielded his eyes. "I thought you knew."

What? What kind of answer was that?

"Buddy," Sammy barked at him again. "Are you drunk?"

The stranger's lashes lifted. He stared at Shelly for a moment, and there was no missing the sadness in his eyes. Her heart ached as she gazed at him.

"I don't drink," he told Sammy.

"Then you should probably get your ass out of my bar," Sammy fired back, not missing a beat.

"And stop bothering my customers." His thick, white brows had beetled over his eyes.

The stranger stiffened.

"Sammy, it's okay," Shelly said, her voice soft. "I think he's confused." Her head tilted. She actually thought he was a whole lot more than just confused. "What's your name?"

He hesitated.

"Do you know your name?" Shelly pushed. Now she was really worried for him.

His hand clenched into a fist. "My mistake. Don't...know you. You...don't know me." And then he turned and marched away, clearing a path right through the crowd.

"Hey, buddy!" Sammy yelled after him. "Don't forget your coat!"

Shelly didn't think the guy had a coat. She watched him, unable to look away, until the bar's door closed behind him.

"I need to call the sheriff," Sammy groused. "Something ain't right with that man."

Her gaze shot back to Sammy.

Sammy was still staring at the shut door. "Didn't like the way he looked at you."

"He looked sad," Shelly replied. "I felt—"

"Sorry for him?" Sammy cut in with a knowing nod. "Your heart has always been too soft, baby. That man didn't look sad to me."

She rolled back her shoulders and clutched the keys tighter. "How did he look?"

"He looked desperate. He stared at you like you were his whole damn world, and I'm telling you right now, that shit ain't normal."

***

She didn't know him.

He stood in the shadows, the trees surrounding him and the faint music and voices from the bar drifting across the street to reach his ears. He was over fifty feet away from the bar, but if he focused, he could still hear the conversations *inside* that place. He could hear them all too clearly.

His sense of hearing was enhanced, he knew that. So was his sense of vision. His sense of smell. He wasn't like other men—he'd realized that fact right after he'd escaped from the lab.

A fucking lab. He'd been kept locked away, hidden from the rest of the world. He'd been an experiment. But he'd gotten loose. He'd escaped.

And he'd found…her.

The woman with the long, dark hair. The woman with the eyes that were pure chocolate. The woman with the silken skin and the slow, sweet smile. The woman who stared at him—

As if she'd never seen him in her life.

It's a lie. She knows me. She has to know me.

As he watched, the door to the bar opened. *She* appeared, shivering a bit.

He supposed it was cold. He didn't really feel the cold, though. It didn't matter to him.

She wasn't alone. The old bartender was with her. He was glancing around, looking to the left and right suspiciously.

He's looking for me.

The bartender wouldn't see him, though. He was hidden too well. Cloaked. As he watched, the bartender led the woman to her car. She gave the fellow a hug, and then slipped inside her ride. She cranked her engine as the bartender turned away, hunching his shoulders.

She has to know me. He waited in the shadows, absolutely still in his hiding space, until the bartender went back inside. His prey hadn't left yet. Her car lights were on.

If you wanted to keep her safe, you should have waited until she drove away before you left her. But the cold had driven the old man inside too fast and now…

Now, I can have her.

In an instant, he'd left his hiding space. He cleared the distance between them in mere seconds. He was faster than a normal man.

Because I'm not normal.

He was beside her car before she could even shift gears. He rapped on the window, and she gave a scream.

He stiffened. He didn't like her scream. He didn't like her fear. Raising his voice so she could hear him through the glass, he said, "I'm not going to hurt you."

Her head whipped toward the window. She stared at him with absolute terror clear on her beautiful face.

He needed to think. He had to show her that he wasn't a threat. That everything was okay. He held up his hands. "I just want to talk with you." She *had* to know who he was.

This woman—she had been in his head every single day since he'd woken in the lab. He'd woken up to find himself strapped down on an exam table. He'd been confused as all hell, but the woman in the car—she'd come to him. She'd slipped into his dreams. Walked into his fantasies. She'd possessed him.

His past was gone. He didn't know his name. Didn't know where he'd come from. Didn't know who the hell his family was. The *only* thing he remembered about his time before that lab...the only thing he remembered was her.

She was the key to his past.

She had to help him.

"Please." The word was too rough and hard as it burst from him. "I need your help."

But she was afraid. And there was...

His nostrils flared.

There was a hard, bitter scent in the air. He inhaled again, and his whole body stiffened.

"Get out of the car!" he roared at her.

She didn't get out. She shoved the car into reverse and it zoomed back, narrowly missing his foot.

He grabbed for the door, holding tightly. "Get out!"

But she wasn't listening. She'd shifted gears again, and her car lurched forward even as the bitter, acidic scent got stronger. Something was wrong with her vehicle. Very, very wrong. But she wasn't listening to him. She was driving away, and he was chasing after her. He was fast, but he wasn't faster than a car. Shit, *shit*. He glanced around, frantic, and saw a man with a baseball cap jumping out of a black pickup truck. The truck's engine was still running, so he didn't hesitate. He shoved the guy with the cap out of his way as he leapt into that truck. Then he raced away, chasing after her small, blue car.

His heart pounded too fast. His hands clenched the steering wheel. His gut was in knots, and he could have sworn that he felt...fear?

Was this what fear felt like? This bitterness on his tongue? The tenseness of his muscles?

He saw her car up ahead. She was going too fast as she headed into a turn. She needed to brake, and her tail lights flashed as if she were *trying* to brake, but her car didn't slow down.

She narrowly avoided driving her vehicle right over the edge of the mountain road. And the drop had to be several hundred damn feet.

Her brakes aren't working. That's what I smelled. Brake fluid. Oh, fucking hell. He'd traveled that road hours before while he searched for her. While he'd been *pulled* toward her. He'd hitchhiked his way to the mountain town in order to find her. And he knew an even worse turn waited up the road. If she couldn't brake, if she lost control because she was going too fast...

He shoved down his gas pedal. He had to stop her. Had to find a way to help her. He passed her car and for an instant, she turned her head to look at him. There was absolute desperation on her face.

He pulled over in front of her. Slowed his vehicle. Her car hit him, plowing into the truck's bumper. He lurched forward at the impact, but kept his grip steady on the wheel. She hit him again. Bumping hard and his head snapped forward. He clenched his teeth and hit the brakes, going slower, slower, easing up until his truck was stopped...and she was, too.

Until she was safe.

They'd managed to stop right before what he thought of as the death curve. Sonofabitch.

He killed the engine and popped the parking brake. Then he jumped out of the truck. Ran toward her. She threw open her door. She raced out of her car, and her hair flew around her shoulders as she came to a quick halt. "My brakes wouldn't work! I couldn't stop—"

"Your brakes were damaged. I could smell brake fluid back at the bar—"

Her breath came in rough, desperate pants. He swore that he could hear the frantic beating of her heart. "Did you do it?" she demanded.

"What? No!" He took a quick step toward her.

She immediately backed away.

"I could smell the brake fluid." He fought to keep his voice calm. "That's why I was telling you to get out of the car when we were in the parking lot. I knew something was wrong."

Her gaze jumped from him to the truck. "How did you do that? How did you stop me?"

He had no real fucking clue. Well, okay, he partially knew. One of his new bonuses was that he had incredibly fast reflexes. He'd leapt into that truck and desperation had taken over. "Figured if I could get in front of you, I could stop us both."

Her eyes were huge. "You could have been hurt."

At that, he smiled. "It takes an awful lot to hurt me."

A faint snap reached his ears. A twig...breaking? His head whipped to the left, and he stared into the darkness of the trees. His body had gone on high alert.

Danger.

"Get down," he growled.

"What? Why?"

A whistle reached him—the sound of air rushing too fast.

He didn't hesitate. He lunged toward her, threw his body onto hers, and they both slammed into the ground.

She was shaking and she was...warm. Soft. Her scent—sweet, feminine—teased his nostrils.

"Get off me!" She pushed against him.

But he didn't move. "Sh-shooter..." Why was talking suddenly so hard for him?

"What?" But then she gave a little scream. "You're bleeding!" Her hands were sliding over his body. "I can feel your blood!"

Because that whistling he'd heard...it had been a bullet. One that was aimed at her. Someone was trying to kill her. Someone was trying to take her from him. "St-stay down..."

In the distance, he could hear a siren. The owner of the truck he'd stolen had probably called in the local cops. They were going to hunt him down. And if they hunted him, they'd find her. Help was coming. She just had to stay safe long enough for it to arrive.

"Shooter..." he whispered. "In the woods..."

"OhmyGod." Her hands stilled on him. She stared up at him, and even in the dark, he could see her perfectly. "You were just shot protecting me?"

Didn't she get it? Didn't she know…?

He forced out the words. "Die…for you."

She shook her head. "No, you absolutely will not. You don't even *know* me. You are not going to die for me. People don't die for strangers, okay? Haven't you watched the news? That's not the way things work. You don't—"

"Know you…" Talking was too hard. And the cold that he shouldn't feel? He was feeling it right then. His body had gone numb. "You're…the only thing…I know."

"But you don't know me! You don't even know my name!" She shoved against him, but he wouldn't move. He wasn't going to leave her unprotected. "Help!" Her scream filled his ears. "Someone, we need help!"

And help was coming…help was getting ever closer, he could hear those sirens. But…help wouldn't arrive soon enough for him.

The bullet had torn through his back. It was lodged inside of him. It was killing him. "Found you…" he whispered. His head turned and his lips feathered over her cheek. "Found you."

"Help us!"

Her scream was the last thing he heard.

***

"Stay with me!" Shelly grabbed the hand of the man who'd saved her life — the stranger with the dark hair and the piercing blue eyes. The stranger who was still and cold on the stretcher. "Don't you do this!"

The EMTs shared a long look. "Ma'am, you need to let him go."

"You have to help him!" A deputy's car had raced to the scene first. How long ago had that been? Twenty minutes? Half an hour ago? Once he'd arrived, the guy had radioed for help, and the ambulance had come, but the ambulance attendants weren't helping! "Stop the bleeding! I think the bullet is still inside of him! You need to —"

"He's gone, Shelly."

She stiffened. Her gaze jerked to the right. The sheriff stood there, lit by the swirl of lights. His hat was pulled low over his head, and his hands were on his lean hips. His badge gleamed.

"He was dead before the ambulance arrived," the sheriff added softly, his lips tightening. "I'm sorry."

She was still clutching the stranger's hand. She didn't even know his name. He'd saved her — *twice* — and he was dead? Just dead? This couldn't happen! It wasn't right.

"Let him go," Sheriff Blane Gallows added. "They need to take him away."

She didn't want to let him go. She wanted him to open his eyes. To see her.

Found you.

"Shelly, I know this isn't easy, but you *have* to let the man go now." The sheriff's voice was soft, tender. She'd known Blane her whole life. She'd spent many summers and holidays in the mountains, and they'd grown up together. Been friends, even tried a brief period of time being lovers. That hadn't worked, but they'd remained close.

"I don't even know his name," she whispered. He should feel cold, shouldn't he? He was dead, she was holding onto a dead man, but his skin still felt warm to her.

"He didn't have ID," Blane told her, his hand squeezing her shoulder. "But we can get his prints. We'll figure out who he was. Notify his family. Don't worry, we'll take care of him."

She made herself let him go. Shelly turned her head and met Blane's green gaze. "He saved my life."

Determination sharpened his features. "We're looking for the hunter who fired that shot. Damn fools can't understand regulations…"

Shelly shivered. She wasn't so sure the shot had been fired by a reckless hunter. "My brakes didn't work. He saved me—God, I guess he saved me twice." She looked back at the stranger, helpless, but he'd just been loaded into the ambulance. His face had been covered, his body covered.

Found you. His rumbling voice echoed in her mind.

"Come on, Shelly, I'll take you to the cabin," Blane promised her. "It's too cold to stay out here."

Shoulders hunching, Shelly nodded. Blane was right. There was no point in staying out there any longer. The mysterious stranger who'd saved her life—he was gone.

A light dusting of snow began to fall.

And a tear slid down her cheek.

***

His eyes opened and, at first, he only saw a wall of white. He jerked upright as he realized that some sort of cover was over him—a sheet? *What the fuck?* He shoved it out of his way and glanced around.

Someone screamed. Over and over again.

A woman. She had a stethoscope around her neck and she wore some kind of blue uniform. She gaped at him, her eyes huge and her face stark white. "You're dead!" she yelled. "Dead, dead—"

A quick sweep of his gaze revealed that he was in the back of an ambulance. The vehicle gave a sharp swerve to the left, and he knew the driver had heard the woman's screams.

"Not exactly," he muttered, and he leapt for the back doors. He shoved those doors open even as the ambulance fish-tailed, and he jumped out, flying right from the rear of the vehicle. He didn't fall. Didn't stumble at all. He landed on his feet, and he took off running for the line of trees. He heard the screech of the ambulance braking behind him. And he also heard —

"*Dead! He's dead!*" The woman was still screaming.

She was…not wrong.

It wasn't the first time he'd woken from the dead. And he feared it wouldn't be his last, either.

CHAPTER TWO

It was midnight, and Shelly still couldn't sleep. She paced the confines of her cabin, her bare feet sliding over the old, wood floors. She'd tried to sleep, but every single time that she'd closed her eyes, she'd seen her stranger. She'd seen him dying, for her.

The fire crackled in the large, stone fireplace. The red and orange flames were dancing as she stared straight at them. Guilt twisted her stomach. The same guilt had her hands shaking in front of her. A man had died, and she was so sick of death. Sick of it reaching for the people around her, over and over again. Sick of —

A soft knock sounded at her door. Her head jerked toward the sound, and her brows lowered as she gazed at the door. She was near the top of the mountain, on an isolated, private stretch of land. Land that had been in her family for generations.

The knock came again, only harder this time. Stronger.

Shelly swallowed as she inched toward the door. It was too late for a visitor. The place was too isolated for some tourist to wander up to her doorstep by mistake. Her phone was on the table near the door, and she grabbed it. Her fingers swiped over the screen. She could call Blane and get the sheriff there in…

In thirty minutes. Because that's how long it takes to get from his place to the top of this mountain. Oh, damn.

The knock came again. Harder. And…

"I know you're in there." A man's voice. Strong. Familiar. "You're standing behind the door, and you're scared, but you don't need to be."

No, no way. *No.* She was wrong about the voice being familiar. Wrong because it *couldn't* be, could *not* be—

Her stranger?

She surged toward the door, flipped the locks and yanked the door open. A cold burst of wind and snow hit her, and Shelly stared in shock at the man before her.

It was him. Her stranger.

The hero.

The *dead* man.

Her knees started to buckle. The phone slipped from her grasp and dropped to the floor. She was about to follow that phone and hit the wooden floor, but—but he caught her. He moved so fast, catching her and lifting her into his arms. He held her easily as he swept into her cabin, kicking the door shut behind him.

She should scream. She should jerk out of his arms. She should do *something*.

"You should breathe," he told her, and his lips — firm, sensual — kicked up just a bit. "That's what you should do first. Breathe. Then you can scream. You can jerk away from me. You can do everything else you have planned, but you have to start by breathing."

He carried her to the chair in front of her fireplace. He sat her down ever so carefully even as she sucked in a couple of deep gulps of air.

He knelt in front of her, his hands going to cage her in the chair. His hair was mussed and dusted by a bit of snow. His eyes were just as amazingly blue as they'd been before. He wore a t-shirt — the same black t-shirt he'd worn at the bar. Jeans. Boots.

"You're dead," Shelly said.

"I actually get that a lot."

"What?"

His right hand moved to cup her cheek. His touch was so warm, and she flinched against him.

"Easy." His gaze didn't leave her. "I just want to make sure you're not going to pass out on me."

Her hand caught his. Held tight. "You're here. Really here."

One dark eyebrow raised. "Yes."

"I'm not dreaming? Hallucinating? Having some kind of breakdown?" Shelly needed to be one hundred percent sure of this.

All trace of amusement left his face. "I'm right here."

She shook her head. "I saw you die."

He glanced away from her.

She was still holding his hand. Still holding him, and Shelly didn't think she'd ever let go. "Who are you?"

He swallowed. "I really hoped you'd know."

What? "I'm Shelly. Shelly Hampton, and I wish that I could say I knew you, but I'm sorry, I don't."

"Shelly." He seemed to taste her name. Savor it.

She shivered.

His gaze focused on her once more. "I need to tell you some things. And when I do, I want you to promise me that you'll keep taking those deep breaths, okay?"

She sucked in another deep gulp of air.

"The things I say, they're going to sound crazy, but I swear, they are true. I'm not lying to you. I *won't* lie to you."

His voice was so deep and hard. His gaze so intense.

"I don't know who I am." His gaze held hers. "A few months ago, I woke up in a lab. I was strapped to an exam table. Men and women in white coats rushed around me. I heard them saying my experiment was a success."

She pulled in another breath.

"They kept me locked away in a facility — didn't take me long to figure out it was run by the government. They thought I couldn't hear them when they talked, didn't think I picked up on their whispers, but I did. They said the place was part of Project Lazarus, and I was a test subject. A fucking lab rat to them."

She had no idea where this story was going. She didn't —

"Then they killed me."

"What?"

He rolled back his shoulders and surged to his feet. His hand pulled from her hold as he towered over her. "I think they killed me five times. Part of their experiment, you see. Because they wanted to see how long it would take me to come back from the dead."

She could only stare at him. *I'm in the mountains, alone in my cabin, with a man who is insane. I let him in my home. Does that make me crazy, too? It must, it —*

"You're not fucking crazy," he growled. "And you're also not remembering to breathe, Shelly. *Breathe.*"

She sucked in more air. Her heart was racing so fast she thought it might burst from her chest at any moment.

"I hate that you're afraid of me. I-I didn't think you'd be afraid." He raked his hand through his hair. "I thought you'd see me...that you'd *know* me."

"Um." She cleared her throat. "Excuse me, but I have to tell you that we've never met. Never. I mean, not before I saw you in the bar tonight. We're strangers."

His whole body stiffened. "We can't be." His hand dropped to his side. For an instant, fury was on his face, and his lethal glare had fear surging even stronger inside of her. She pressed back into the chair and tried to figure out how she could escape. How she—

"You can't run from me." A muscle jerked in his jaw. "I'm here to protect you. You're in danger, don't you see that?"

She was seeing that fact pretty clearly. Because the guy in front of her was spinning some wild story about a government experiment and—

"You were in my mind. From the minute I woke up in that hell, you were in my head. I'd have flashes of you. I couldn't remember anything else, only *you*." He was definitely angry. He spun away from her, pacing toward the fire.

"You were — you *are* the only thing I know, and you stare at me like I'm a monster."

Time for her to run. While his back was turned. *Now.* Shelly leapt from the chair and raced for the door. Her hands flew out and —

Hit him.

Because the big, probably crazy stranger was suddenly in front of her. Impossible. He'd been *behind* her. He'd been in front of the fireplace. But now he was between her and the door. He'd *beaten* her to the door. And he wasn't even breathing hard.

"I am not here to hurt you. You're in danger, but not from me." His voice was low, and it seemed to sink right beneath her skin. "I found you...I tracked you...I searched for you because I knew I had to keep you safe."

"But you *don't* know me." Her voice was too high. Cracking. A terrible contrast to his. "We don't know each other."

Pain flashed in his eyes but was quickly masked. "You are the only thing I know. They held me in their lab, kept me prisoner for months. Experimented on me again and again. Killing me, bringing me back."

No, surely...

Dear God, that couldn't be true, could it? "Y-you were shot tonight. Show me your back."

Staring straight at her, he yanked the shirt over his head.

She swallowed. Twice. The guy was *built*. He didn't just have a six pack going on. More like a twelve pack. But there were scars on his chest. Faint white ridges. A lot of them. Bullet wounds? Knife wounds?

He turned, giving her his back.

And where there *should* have been a gaping hole...her fingers reached out and touched warm skin. He jerked hard beneath her touch, and she heard him hiss out a rough breath. "Got the bullet out. I'm okay now."

She didn't stop touching him. His skin was...it was slightly red in the middle of his back, near his spine, and she could have sworn that what looked like some kind of fresh scar tissue was starting to form. "Impossible." Was that...was that blood still on his back? Dried blood?

He turned toward her. Offered her the shirt in his hand.

Shaking, she took the shirt and she found the hole that had been left by the bullet. There was dried blood on the shirt. *His* blood. She dropped the shirt. Backed up four quick steps. Shook her head. "This *isn't* happening."

"I wish it fucking weren't. It's my life, though. Or what's left of it." He gave a grim laugh. "*You're* what's left of it. I found you."

Those words—Oh, God.

"I knew you were out there. You were in my head, and I knew you had to be real, no matter what bullshit the assholes in that lab told me. When the place was destroyed, I escaped. I came looking for you." He advanced toward her.

Shelly backed up another step.

"You're in danger." His hands fisted at his sides. "I know it. I can...I can sense things, okay? Hell, I can come back from the dead. I think that proves I'm not exactly normal."

No, he was far from normal.

"My senses are better than a normal man's. Far fucking better. I can hear through walls, I can hear whispers from a hundred yards away. I can see better than any human—see, hear, smell. I'm faster, I'm stronger."

Nothing he was saying reassured her. "How do I know that you aren't just crazy?"

His eyes narrowed. "I can prove it."

Um...

A moment later, he opened the cabin's front door. Cold air blew inside, chilling her. "Come and watch," he invited.

And then he slipped outside. She rushed to the door, intending to slam it shut and *lock* him out while she still had the chance. This was her perfect opportunity, this was—

He was gone.

Her head poked out of the doorway. She looked to the left, to the right, but he wasn't there. He'd vanished in a blink. No way. Impossible.

Shut the door. Go inside. Lock him out —

"A lock won't keep me out." His voice boomed in the night. Boomed — and he had to be a good hundred yards away from her. She inched forward onto her porch, squinting to try and make him out in the distance. He was a shadowy figure and —

Then the shadowy figure seemed to *fly* toward her. He moved so fast. She opened her mouth to scream, and he was just there. Right in front of her. Touching her. Holding her.

"Told you," he said, his voice eerily calm. "I'm fast."

And he let her go. He backed away. An old tree had fallen near her house. The tree's trunk had to be at least five feet round. He grabbed the tree and lifted it up, as if it weighed nothing.

Oh, God.

She ran back into the cabin. Slammed the door. Locked the door. Triple locked it. Her right foot hit the phone she'd dropped moments before, and she yanked it up. Her fingers flew over the screen as she started to call Blane —

The door burst open.

She yelped and whirled to face the man standing there. He'd knocked in her door — and he still held up one hand, as if he'd just used *one hand* to break into her cabin.

Shelly rushed across the room, she grabbed for the fireplace poker, but he was too fast. He got to the fireplace first. His hands closed around hers before she could get a weapon. The phone went flying again as he pulled her close.

"Don't hurt me," she cried even as she tried to figure out how to hurt *him.*

But his eyes widened in absolute shock. "Never," he swore, and his hold — it was careful. Gentle. His fingers were around her wrists, but his thumbs were stroking her skin. "I came to keep you safe, not to hurt you."

He *had* saved her life — twice. Shelly's head tilted as she fought her fear and studied him. "You really don't know who you are?"

He shook his head. "In the lab, they just gave me a number. Never used a name. And like I said, the only thing about my past that I remember —"

"Is me," she finished softly. Her words were calm and quiet, but her heart was racing like crazy in her chest. What he said didn't make a bit of sense to her. Everything seemed impossible but...

But...

She had seen him die. He'd been dead at the crash scene on the mountain road. And she'd seen his super speed. His incredible strength. "Is there anything else you can do? Any other super powers that I need to know about?" Because, yes, it sounded like she was boarding the crazy train.

His gaze cut away from her.

Oh, crap. "There *is* something else."

He kept stroking her inner wrists. Her pulse was going mad beneath his touch. Understandable since he scared her. A guy with his powers, how could he not scare her? But there was also a strange awareness between them. A sort of primitive pulse that was drawing her to him.

Desire. Lust.

The guy was drop-dead sexy. She'd never been the type to fall for a tall, dark stranger, especially not one who came with all of his extra features.

Only she wasn't pulling away from him. She was standing there, enjoying his touch despite the madness that he'd brought her way.

Maybe she was the crazy one. Shelly cleared her throat. "What aren't you telling me?" Her head tilted back more as she stared up at him. "Can you fly? Because if you can fly —"

"I can't fly." His gaze came back to hers, and it actually seemed to — to heat. A sensual awareness filled his stare. "But I am tuned to you."

"Okay, I don't know what that means. Seriously, no idea."

"It means that I can feel you. How the hell do you think I found you in these mountains? It's like — hell, it's so hard to explain, but it's like an invisible thread connects me to you. When I broke out of that lab, I could feel it. I could feel it when I was still *in* the lab, too. It's a pull that leads me straight to you." He hesitated, and she knew there was more. Only she wasn't so certain she wanted to know the rest. Maybe she'd had enough revelations for one night.

An invisible pull? Was the guy saying he could basically, what? Find her, anywhere she went? That was —

"When your thoughts are strong enough and I...think when we're physically close, I can hear them." Another confession from him.

Her jaw dropped.

"So, yeah, I can find you anywhere. I can — "

"I-I didn't say that part out loud." She yanked her hands back from him.

He frowned at her. "You don't have to pull away. I like touching you, too. I feel the desire, too. I wanted you before I even knew if you were real or just a figment of my desperation, and I — "

I feel the desire, too. No, no, he *knew* that she felt that weird attraction to him? Now her cheeks were burning hot, and not because of the flames in the fireplace. "You don't just jump into someone's head. You don't do that. It is *not* appropriate."

His frown deepened as his brows pulled low. "I was just trying to understand you. I knew you were afraid, and I wanted to see if you could feel anything other than fear for—"

She jabbed her index finger into his chest. His bare chest. His sexy chest. *Focus.* "Do *not* get into my head again, do you understand me? Because I am trying hard not to have an absolute freak-out on you. You're some kind of superman who has just landed on my doorstep, and on top of all the other terrible shit in my life, I don't know if I can handle this right now." *I don't know if I can handle you.*

He blinked. "I told you, I'm here to help you. I think you're in danger. After what happened tonight, I *know* you are—"

"Blane—Sheriff Blane Gallows said some hunter accidentally fired at us, and Blane told me that my brakes had gone out because of a leak. Wear and tear. No one was gunning for me. No one was—"

His hand curled around hers. But he didn't move her hand away from his body. Instead, he flattened her palm against his chest, and she could feel the thunder of his heartbeat. "That wasn't a hunter firing at you. The shot came from far away, from a guy who knew how to use a scope and aim perfectly in the dark. Probably a trained sniper. He'd picked that spot deliberately because he expected you to go off the mountain there. He knew your brakes couldn't handle the turn. He was there, waiting, to finish off the job, just in case you managed to get out of your car before it went over the edge."

She licked lips that had gone far too dry.

He gave a low growl. A sound that was weirdly sexy. All hard and primal.

Her breasts tightened. *What is wrong with me?* She cleared her throat. "You can't know that."

He just stared at her. "I could hear the shot coming. I was able to figure out the guy's location. A sniper spot. After he hit me, I heard him flee. If I hadn't been dying, I would have given chase."

Dying. "Y-you knew you'd come back." Come back from the dead. Was she seriously saying this stuff?

He gave a little shrug. "I figured the odds were good."

"What if you hadn't?" Her voice was husky. "What if you'd died right there and that had just been the end?"

"Then you'd still be alive."

She snatched her hand back. "Don't." Her whole body had gone tense. "Do not *ever* do something like that again, got me? Because I don't want someone dying for me."

He blinked. Seemed confused. Fair enough— that made two of them.

She needed to put some distance between her and her mystery man. "You should leave."

He glanced toward her door. Her *broken* door. "It's not safe for you to be alone out here. You're being targeted." He rolled back his shoulders. "I'll fix your door." He hesitated. "I can...I can stay outside, if you'll let me. The cold doesn't do anything to me, and—"

"You're not staying outside." A terrible thought struck her. But if everything else he'd said was true...*oh, jeez.* "You don't have any place to go, do you?"

He gave a curt shake of his head. A negative shake.

Was she really supposed to kick out the man who'd saved her? Turn him out into the cold, winter night? Shelly bit her lower lip. Dammit. "This cabin is plenty big enough for us both." No, she hadn't just said that.

Had she?

His eyes widened. "You'd let me stay with you?"

Her breath heaved out. "The place has three floors, okay? Plenty of room. I'm on the top floor. You can take this one. Use the bathroom. Shower off the blood. And get a good night's sleep. We can figure out everything else in the morning." She paused. "Don't go down to the lower floor, okay? It's, um, locked up." Partially true—her studio was down there, and she wasn't up to going in that particular room yet.

He wasn't even blinking. Maybe she'd made a huge mistake. Maybe he was some kind of serial killer and this was a terrible—

"I'm not a serial killer," he gritted out.

Her hands flew up. "Stay out of my head!" *Everything he said is true.* She'd need more than a few hours of sleep to wrap her mind around all of that. "That's the number one rule between us, okay? Don't jump in my head. You saved my life, so I owe you." Seriously owed him. "You can stay here and I'll...I'll try to help you."

For an instant, hope flashed on his face. It was almost painful to see.

"I don't know you." She bit her lower lip. "I don't know how you know me. How you remember me, but after everything that's happened, I will help you. I'll help you try and figure out who you are."

"Thank you."

She gave him a weak smile.

His face tensed. His eyes glittered even more.

"Um, is everything all right?" Shelly asked him as she tucked a lock of hair behind her ear.

"I want you."

Her heart thudded into her chest.

"You...want me, too." Now he was the one clearing his throat, but it didn't seem to help because when he talked again, his voice was still more like a growl than anything else. "I picked up that thought *before* you told me to stay out of your head."

Her cheeks burned again as she blushed. "I don't make a habit of sleeping with men I've just met." *And I don't even know your name!* She'd have to start calling him something soon. Shelly pointed down the hallway. "After you fix the door…" And really, he'd broken it so it only seemed fair that he fix it, right? Not like she was asking for too much. "Use the bedroom and the bathroom on the right." She hurried toward the stairs. Shelly knew she needed to get away from her stranger. Maybe put a few locked doors between them.

Then again, he didn't seem to have any trouble knocking down locked doors.

"We can talk in the morning," Shelly added, throwing those words over her shoulder. Her hand slid up the wooden banister. She didn't look back, not until she reached the upper floor. She paused then, leaning a bit over the wooden balcony. And she found his gaze right on her. For a moment, she absolutely could not look away. There was just something about him. So intense, so powerful…

I don't know him. We've never met. Because there was no way she could ever forget a man like him.

No way.

***

He hadn't forgotten her.

Shelly moved away from the wooden balcony. Her soft steps padded over the carpet, and then he heard the faint sound of her door shutting—and the click of the lock sliding into place.

He still didn't move.

She's real. I touched her. I spoke to her. The doctors at the lab had tried to tell him that he'd just imagined her. They'd been so certain that he couldn't remember the woman with the long, dark hair and the deep, dark eyes. They'd been so certain he was wrong. They'd pumped him with drugs—hell, sometimes, he'd been sure they were *trying* to make him forget her.

But he hadn't forgotten her. She was the only thing he remembered. The only thing that mattered. And every instinct he had screamed that she was in trouble.

Shelly.

His Shelly.

He found some tools in the garage just beyond the cabin. He fixed her door, discovered that the task was surprisingly easy. Maybe he'd been some kind of handyman in his former life.

He put the tools away and as he walked toward the room Shelly had indicated, he saw her phone on the floor. Frowning, he picked it up, and when he did, the screen glowed, showing him a picture of a blond man. A man who had his arm wrapped around Shelly.

Anger churned inside of him. *Who in the hell is that asshole?* His fingers swiped over the screen and her contact list came up. The guy...he was Blane Gallows.

Sheriff Blane Gallows. Shelly had said that.

She'd been...attempting to call Blane? When she'd been so afraid? He looked upstairs. No sound came from her room. Her call hadn't gone through. He didn't have to worry about the sheriff storming to the cabin.

But did he have to worry about the sheriff having some kind of claim on Shelly? Carefully, he put the phone down on a nearby table. With the tension pounding through his body, he was worried he might crush it. He had to always watch himself. He was so strong that he could break things too easily.

I'll have to be extra careful with Shelly.

Because he would never, fucking *ever*, want to break her.

He headed for the bathroom. As he entered the room, he stripped. When he climbed into the shower a few moments later, the hot water poured down on him. He closed his eyes, putting his face under the spray, and in his mind, he saw...her. Only Shelly wasn't in the cabin any longer.

She was walking on a beach. Her hair blew in the breeze behind her. Shelly wore a small, blue bikini, one that showed off her perfect curves. She stopped walking and stared off into the distance. Her feet curled into the sand and then a wave came up and tickled her toes.

She laughed. The sound pierced right through him. She laughed and then she turned…

I swear, she turned to look at me.

The image disappeared from his mind. The waves were gone, and all he knew was the pounding rush of the shower's water. Frustration surged within him. He wanted the fucking surf back. He wanted the damn beach. He wanted Shelly in her bikini.

He wanted his life.

CHAPTER THREE

Shelly could smell bacon. Eggs. She paused outside of her bedroom, her body tensing even as the tempting aromas filled her nose. She'd always been such a bacon addict. Her bare feet inched forward. She'd showered and dressed, putting on jeans and an oversized, green sweater. She'd wondered if her mystery guy would still be in the cabin. She'd crept out of her room, but then stopped cold when she realized that yes, he was there.

A quick beat of rock music had her hurrying down the stairs. She knew that music. It was actually a ring tone that she'd reserved for Blane. Her phone was on the table near her repaired door, and she quickly scooped it up. "Blane?"

"Shelly!" A bit of static crackled on the line. "Shelly, there's something you need to know…"

Sunlight peeked through her curtains, faint rays because dawn had just arrived.

"Your hero from last night?" Blane continued grimly. "The guy disappeared."

She heard a clatter in the kitchen. She inched toward the sound. Saw her mystery man. *Her hero.* He was only wearing his jeans. He turned toward her, and a quick smile lit his face.

Her heart immediately jumped into a double-time rhythm.

"I've had men searching for him all night. The guy leapt out of the ambulance, and he ran into the woods." Blane's words were gruff, tired. *Because he's been up all night.* "With his injuries, the poor fellow is probably dead out there."

"I thought he was dead before..."

"No, probably was just *near* death. That's what the EMTs figure. He woke up, confused, disoriented, and he fled. God, I wish we could have found the bastard."

The bastard in question put bacon and a pile of eggs onto one of the plates that he'd already set on her kitchen table. Two plates. One for him. One for her.

"I ran his prints—they were all over the inside of that stolen truck. And you aren't going to believe this...Shit, I know it's probably a mistake but—"

She turned away from her mystery man, hunching her shoulders. "You know his name." Excitement made her voice too sharp.

Behind her, well, there was just dead silence.

If he could hear through walls, if he could hear whispers from a hundred yards away, she figured her stranger could overhear every word of her conversation with Blane.

"The prints matched up to a John Smith."

John Smith? For real? That sounded like a fake name to her. An obviously fake name.

"He was a decorated Army Ranger. Served two tours before he went into the private sector. According to what I could gather, the man was a serious bad ass."

She slanted a glance over her shoulder. The bad ass in her kitchen had frozen. His gaze was locked on her.

"But he died," Blane added grimly. "He was stabbed by an unknown assailant. The guy was working some kind of private security gig in Miami. Things went south, and he wound up dead in an alley."

A chill skated over her skin. The chill came both from the fact that Blane had said that John Smith was a dead man and from the fact that the guy had died in Miami. *She* lived in Miami. The city was her home base.

"I'll keep the search crews looking for him." Blane exhaled on a long sigh. "We'll find the guy's body, bring him in. Figure out who the hell he *really* is because there must have been some mix-up with the prints in that truck."

She didn't think there had been a mix-up. And she didn't want Blane to continue searching needlessly. Why waste that time and manpower

when the missing guy was right in front of her?
"Blane, he's—"

Right in front of me. The stranger—John?—had
moved with that super speed of his, and he was
literally right in front of her. And his hand—his
hand was over her mouth.

He leaned in toward her, and his lips
brushed over her ear as he said, "Don't tell him
I'm here." His voice was so low. Barely a breath
against her left ear.

She shivered.

"Shelly?" Blane blasted. The phone was still
at her right ear. "Everything okay? I don't have
the best connection with you."

No, calls in the mountains were always
terrible. John's hand slid away from her mouth.

John. I can start calling him John. She licked her
lips. "I'm okay."

"I'll call you later, all right? Got some men
waiting on me." And then he was gone. Blane
had ended the call before she could say anything
else.

John took the phone from her. He put it on
the counter. He stared at her with his incredible
eyes. "I'm not going to hurt you."

Her chin notched up. "Why are you saying
that?"

"Because you looked scared as hell of me,
and I'm trying to reassure you."

Her gaze slid over his body. Over the faint scar marks. "Being in the military would fit. I mean, it would fit with your scars. Some of them look like bullet wounds. Maybe even...knife slices?" Her gaze rose and she found that his stare was still on her. "And your hair looks like a military cut."

"I like it short," he muttered. "Your...*friend*...the sheriff thinks I'm John Smith."

"He thinks there was a mix-up with the fingerprints. John Smith is a dead man."

Now he laughed. The sound was rusty, but deep. Sexy. "That's the truth." He turned away from her, his broad back moving away as he motioned toward the table. "Since you gave me a place to stay, I figured the least I could do was make breakfast. I know how much you like bacon, so when I found a pack in the fridge, I went ahead and prepared it all. I also put extra milk in your coffee, because you like—"

"How do you know that?" She was rooted to the spot.

His hand lowered and his fingers curled around the back of a nearby chair.

"You said you only remembered me." It was an effort to keep her voice at a semi-calm level. "And I'm trying to follow along, I swear, I am. But *how* do you know I like bacon? That I put extra milk in my coffee, that—"

"That you have a half-moon birth mark on your right hip?" He looked back at her. "That you like to read every single night before you go to bed? That you curl up with a patchwork quilt in a condo that overlooks the Miami beach, and you read until you fall asleep?"

Her heart seemed to have stopped beating.

"I don't know." He shook his head. "I wish like hell that I did. I know all the details about your life, but not a damn thing about my own."

She should probably run from him. Race away as fast as she could. Not that she'd be faster than him. John...he really wasn't like other men. And pretending all of this stuff wasn't real, that it was just some crazy dream — well, that wasn't going to work. So she took a step toward him. Then another. And her hand reached out to touch his arm. Still so warm, warmer than her own skin. "You're John Smith."

His gaze was fixed on her.

"We have a name. That's something to work with. We can use the computer in the den. I mean, come on, it's the social media age. There has to be a picture out there. We can look at the picture and compare it to you. John Smith, in Miami." Okay, sure, John Smith was *way* too common of a name, but it was a starting point. She squeezed his arm. "You were in the military. A Ranger. You were one of the good guys."

"Are you sure I'm good?"

She forced herself to smile at him. "You'd better be. Or else I'm in some serious trouble."

He didn't smile back at her. Instead, he turned his body toward her, and the hand that had been gripping the back of the chair rose. His knuckles trailed over her cheek. "I can remember everything about you," he rasped. "Except..."

"Except what?"

His gaze fell to her mouth. "I don't remember how you taste."

Her stomach clenched. "That's because we've never kissed." They'd never *met*. Right?

"I know what you look like when you're barely dressed. When you're walking on a beach wearing a blue bikini and driving me insane."

Over the spring and summer, she'd worn her blue bikini plenty of times in Miami. Perhaps he'd seen her. Maybe they'd even met on the beach. Chatted in one of those quick, hello talks that people had. Could it be as simple as that? No, no, that wouldn't explain how he knew about her coffee or her—

"I'd like to taste you, Shelly."

OhmyGod. "John, *no*." But somewhere inside of her, a little voice whispered, *Yes, please*.

She saw his pupils expand and she *knew* he'd just read her mind. "I told you to stay out." The words burst from her.

He gave a jerky nod. "Breakfast is getting cold."

He backed away from her. Her knees had locked. He pulled out the chair, holding it for her. She was still not moving. And she was still thinking about the fact that, dammit, yes, she did want to know what he tasted like, too. Because there was an awareness between them, a stark desire that she'd never felt before. Primitive. Basic.

So hot that her skin felt singed.

Shelly sat down. He pushed her chair forward and his fingers lingered on her shoulder. "When you're ready for my mouth, tell me." He walked around the table. Sat across from her. Stared at Shelly with glittering eyes. "Because, baby, I've been ready for you a very, very long time."

She didn't speak. Mostly because Shelly didn't know what to say. She grabbed the bacon. She grabbed the eggs. She used her mouth to *eat*. And she tried not to think about just all the things that John Smith would be able to do to her...with his mouth.

***

He had a name. John Smith.
John.

"That's you." Shelly's fingertips were poised over the keyboard. They were in the den, with its tall, sweeping ceiling and the walls made of gleaming wood. She glanced over her shoulder, her gaze worried as it landed on him. "That's definitely you in the picture."

They'd pulled up an obituary for John Smith of Miami. A short and simple piece that stated the thirty-three-year-old former Army Ranger had been killed in an unsolved attack. The picture of him—well, the picture appeared to be a few years old, but Shelly was right.

It sure as hell was him.

"Your parents are dead." Her voice was soft. "And you don't have any siblings or other relatives listed. I'm…I'm sorry."

His temples were pounding. His gut was twisting, and he had more fucking questions than ever before. "How does a dead man in Miami…how does he end up in some government lab?"

She bit her lip. Then she started typing on the computer again. "Lazarus, right? That's what you said?"

"Yes. Project Lazarus." He'd heard the whispers.

She searched and searched online, but Shelly didn't turn up anything. He could practically feel her frustration. It matched his own. "We need more help," she finally said. "I'll call Blane. Tell him about you. He's the sheriff, so he'll have pull that we can use."

John stiffened at the mention of the other man's name. "I don't think so."

But she jumped to her feet and whirled to face him. "Why the hell not? Look, we can't just leave a search party looking for you endlessly. We'll go to Blane, we'll tell him—"

"That I'm a dead man walking? That I've got super speed, super hearing, that I'm some kind of super freak?" John demanded. *John.* The name still felt odd but it was better than not being anyone at all. "He'll call in his contacts, all right, and the same government assholes who locked me up before will swoop in again. I won't go back to that hell. I can't." He couldn't be locked up again. "They *killed* me, Shelly. Killed me so that they could bring me back, and I can't go through that again." Not and keep his sanity.

She held his stare. Nodded. "I understand." There was sympathy on her face. She felt sorry for him. Dammit, he didn't want her pity. He wanted *her.* He'd wanted her for months. A ghost in his head. An obsession that was now right in front of him. He wanted to reach out and take her.

"I won't let them take you, I promise, John."

Her words were sweet, but she had no idea what they were up against. He'd never forget the explosions that had rocked the lab. The attack that had come from nowhere. Another test subject had been there—one that he'd never been allowed to see, but he'd heard the docs talking about her.

Willow.

She'd escaped the wreckage of that lab, too. Only he didn't know what had happened to her. At the time, he'd been jealous of her — Willow got a name.

He got a freaking number. *Twelve.* John cleared his throat. "Someone else was being held there. A woman named Willow. Heard the doctors talking about her. Always wondered…hell, did she experience the same nightmare I did?"

Shelly's hand closed around his arm. He was still just wearing his jeans, and the flesh to flesh contact with her seemed to burn right through him. Did she have any idea how much he craved her touch? He'd been isolated in that lab. Treated like an animal. He barely remembered what it was like to be human, but he was trying. Fucking hell, he was trying…for her.

"We won't tell Blane everything. Just enough that he'll help us." She bit her lower lip. He didn't want her doing that. When she did cute shit like that with her mouth, she made him want to bite, too. "Let's go to town. We need to get you some clothes and supplies, and we can stop by the sheriff's station."

He'd come to her with only the clothes on his back. Humiliation burned through him. "I know I wasn't always like this."

She didn't speak.

"I was normal. Maybe I can be normal again."

Her smile lit her face. Made her dark eyes shine. Made his heart ache. "I've always found normal to be highly over-rated."

His lips parted. He leaned toward her, wanting nothing more than to pull her close, to *feel* the warmth of her against him. She was laughter and light, and she was what he'd dreamed of when he'd been in that lab. When he'd been empty inside, a dead man locked away from the world. She was life. She was everything, and she was right the hell there.

But then her smile disappeared. "John? What's wrong?"

He'd scared her. He'd let his mask slip again. The desperation he felt must have shone on his face. The old guy at the bar had seen his desperation, too. John knew he had. And that was why the man had demanded that John get the hell away from Shelly.

I can't leave her now.

He tried to think. Tried to figure out what to say that would make her forget the stark hunger that must have been on his face. A craving for her. "It's Christmas," he blurted.

Her eyes widened. Then she nodded. "Almost Christmas. We have a few more days."

"But you don't have a tree. No decorations. Nothing here."

Shadows swept over her face. "No, no, I don't." She dropped her hand. "I...um, I haven't had the best year, I guess you could say. My father died. My...my brother, too." Her lower lip trembled. "My mom died when I was just a kid, and they were all I had left. I didn't exactly plan to celebrate this year. I came here to get away from everything back in Miami. This place — it was always my retreat. You know what I mean, right? Everyone needs a safe place and —" She stopped. "Oh, God, I sound like such a bitch. No, you don't know what I mean. I'm sorry, I —"

"I'm sorry about your family." Tension had thickened his body and his temples were pounding. Again, he had that instinctive feeling of danger. The feeling that something was very, very wrong.

"And I'm sorry for everything that's happened to you." She swiped away a tear that had trickled onto her cheek. He didn't like that she was crying. "Christmas was always so happy for me. Putting up the tree without them just didn't seem right."

He nodded. He wanted to pull her close. To hold her. Was that okay? Was that wrong?

Her breath sighed out as her gaze searched his. "But you don't know that, either, do you? You don't remember holidays, good or bad."

"I remember..." His voice was a rasp. "I remember what a holiday is. I know Christmas is trees with twinkling lights. Families exchanging presents. I know that just like I know Halloween is when kids dress up and get candy. I know facts—I don't know my own memories. It's like they were just wiped away."

Another tear slipped down her cheek. He realized that she was crying for him. Before she could brush away the tear, his finger slipped across her cheek, catching the drop. "Don't," he whispered. "Baby, please, don't ever cry for me."

She was right there. Standing in front of him. He was touching her. His dream. His fantasy. He'd lost so much, but she was there. And she meant something to him—hell, she meant everything. If he could just figure out the puzzle pieces.

"You can make new memories," she told him. "You can get your life back."

Could he?

"We'll get Blane to help us. You'll see. He's one of the good guys, too. We can figure this all out."

He wasn't as convinced as she was. His hand lingered against the silk of her cheek. Her scent filled his lungs. He wanted nothing more than to put his mouth on hers but...

Her choice. Always.

He stepped back.

"I-I have an SUV in the garage. Four wheel drive. My brother kept it here and after he passed, I just..." She gave a hard shake of her head. "I know your shirt has a bullet hole in it, but if you can wear it to town, I swear, we'll get more clothes for you once we're there."

Like he cared about a hole in his shirt. What mattered more—her. "The shooter could be in town."

"It...it was a hunter..." Yet Shelly didn't even sound as if she believed those words.

John shook his head. "Someone is targeting you. If we go to town, you stay with me, every second, you understand?"

"What are you? My bodyguard?"

His heart seemed to jerk.

She laughed. "I was just kidding. Though someone with your super skills would make for one killer bodyguard."

You're a killer...

The whisper slid through his head.

"Come on. We should get going before Blane and his crew waste more time searching for a dead man." She hurried toward the door.

But his gaze fell back on the computer. She'd found no hits with Project Lazarus, but they *had* found an obituary for John Smith.

And John Smith…he could read between the lines of the obituary. He'd been a loner, a trained hunter, military through and through.

Someone who knew how to fight. Someone who knew how to kill.

Someone who was very, very dangerous.

And whatever they did to me in that lab, they just made me even more of a weapon.

CHAPTER FOUR

"Holy shit," the sheriff breathed as he surged to his feet. He stood behind his desk, his hand sliding toward the gun holstered on his hip. "You're a dead man."

John moved forward, instantly positioning his body between the sheriff's twitchy trigger finger and Shelly.

"I got men looking for you! And you're right here, in my damn station?"

"Blane, calm down." Shelly slid to John's side. She had her arms crossed over her chest. "He was injured yesterday. He was hurt. He was confused. He found his way to my cabin, and I patched him up."

Blane's eyes doubled. "Patched him up? The man was freaking shot in the back! He should have died—" He hurried toward John. "Instead, he looks totally fine."

John was fine. Better than fine.

"What the actual fuck?" Blane snarled. He glared at John. His green gaze was hard with fury. "How did you get to her cabin? That's over an hour's drive from the scene where you leapt from the ambulance—"

"I'm really fast," John cut in. "I ran there."

"Bullshit. No one is that fast. And no way could you travel that far, on foot, in the cold. You couldn't—"

"Don't be too sure," Shelly muttered.

Blane parted his lips to respond, but Shelly put her hand on his chest.

A growl instantly vibrated in John's throat.

She looked up at him. "What?"

He didn't like her touching the other guy. And something dark and twisting inside of him was flaring to life.

"Buddy, your ass is under arrest," Blane snarled. He yanked up a pair of cuffs and took an aggressive step toward John.

"What? No!" Shelly's voice rose. "He saved my life yesterday! He was confused, so he wandered away from the scene." She shook her head. "He's still confused. I-I think he hit his head. He doesn't even remember his name."

"Does he remember that he stole a truck?" Blane demanded. The guy's face was sharp with his anger.

John didn't like the sheriff. Not one bit. "I could smell her brake fluid in the parking lot of that bar. I took the truck because she needed help. Did you want me to let her die?"

Blane's slightly pointed chin jutted into the air.

"I'll pay for damages to the truck. I'll talk to the owner, I'll smooth things over," Shelly retorted quickly. "But don't arrest him. John needs our help."

Now suspicion was plain to see on the sheriff's face. "I thought you said he didn't remember his name."

Shelly glanced back at John. A quick, nervous glance before she focused on the sheriff once more. "He...you're the one who told us his name was John. John Smith. You got that from the fingerprints left in the truck. After I talked with you on the phone, we pulled up John Smith's picture at my place, and the guy's obituary photo was a match."

"Shelly," Blane snapped out her name.

And John really didn't appreciate the guy's tone.

"We need to talk," Blane continued curtly. "Alone. Right the hell now." He pointed to the door. "Outside, got it, buddy? Stand outside my door." Then he marched toward the door, obviously expecting John to follow him.

He didn't. Instead, his fingers swept down Shelly's arm. He leaned close to her. "Want me to knock out the sheriff?" One good punch would do it.

"No!" Her eyes had gone so wide. "Just go outside. I'll handle this."

He didn't move.

"Please," she whispered.

"I don't like the way he talks to you." And he said that part loud enough for the asshat sheriff to overhear.

Blane gaped at him. "What?"

"Don't snap at her. Watch your ass around her."

"Are you *threatening* me?"

No, he was just giving a warning that the guy should accept.

"Wait outside, John," Shelly urged. "You'll just be a few feet away from me."

Fine. For her. He took his time walking out of the little office. Blane barked for a fresh-faced, redheaded deputy to watch John. What the hell ever. Then the sheriff slammed the door.

Was that supposed to do anything? A closed door? John propped his shoulders against the wall and got ready to listen to Sheriff Blane's "talk" with Shelly. And if that jerk didn't heed John's warning...

I'll be going in there.

***

"Are you insane?" Blane demanded as he paced around his office. He always paced when he was stressed, she remembered that old habit. "I get that your year has been shit, but, seriously, Shelly, you let that bastard *stay* at your place last night?"

She cringed, knowing John would be overhearing every word. "He saved my life —"

"He stole a truck! And I did some checking. Sammy told me that he made you nervous at the bar, that you were scared of him when you first saw the fellow last night."

Aw, crap. She risked a fast glance over her shoulder. "I wasn't afraid of him." That was a wee lie. "I just didn't understand who he was."

Blane stopped pacing and threw his hands into the air. "How do you know who he is now? You said —"

"The fingerprints are right. I think he's John Smith, Army Ranger, formerly of Miami, and I think —"

"John Smith is dead."

She stared at him. "And you thought the guy who saved me was dead last night. Maybe someone else made that mistake with him before. Make a call for me, okay? Contact the authorities down in Miami — see what you can learn about John."

He blinked at her. "What the hell did you just do?"

She didn't understand.

He pointed at her. "Your voice went soft when you said his name. Jesus, Shelly! Do not do this to me."

She could only shake her head. She wasn't following him.

"You did it when we were kids all the time. You'd find some stray — some hurt animal — and you'd take it in! You fell for any sob story that anyone sang to you. Your heart was always too soft, and you were too damn trusting."

She stiffened but didn't deny his accusations. Was it really so wrong to help hurt animals? And people who'd been a bit down on their luck?

"This guy isn't some lost dog! He's not some broke tourist. He's trouble."

Now her spine straightened. "I don't think he is."

Blane gaped at her. Then he drove a hard hand through his blond hair.

"I think he's a man who has been through a lot. I think he's someone who helped me when I really needed help." She nodded. "And now I'm going to help him. If you won't call the Miami PD, then I'll just hire an investigator to help me." She should have done that first. What was the use of having all her family's money if she didn't use it? If she didn't—

"Don't hire a damn investigator," Blane grumbled. "You know I'll do whatever the hell you want. Don't I always? Since we were kids, you had me wrapped around your little finger." He marched closer to her. Blane's hands closed around her shoulders. "I'll check on him, but, seriously, don't let him stay with you. If you feel sorry for the guy, if you think you owe him, then get him a room in town."

But Shelly shook her head. "It's the holidays. You know all of the rooms are booked—"

"I can find him a room. Hell, maybe I can even convince Sammy to let him use the apartment above the bar. Sammy doesn't rent that place out to tourists, so we both know it's empty."

Yes, but...

I want John to stay with me.

"I have to ask him some questions. Figure out what the hell is happening here." Blane squeezed her shoulders. "And I don't want you staying with some would-be psycho."

She winced. "He's not, and don't say things like that when he can hear you."

"He *can't* hear me. He's outside!" Blane let her go. But his glare didn't lessen. "Tell me the guy won't be staying with you tonight."

Shelly didn't like to lie so she kept her mouth shut. She'd actually slept better last night than she had in ages. And the reason? As wild as it might sound, she'd felt safer because John was there. The guy was pretty much an indestructible soldier. How could she not feel safe with him close by? "The last year hasn't been easy," Shelly said, choosing her words carefully. "First my father and his heart attack. Then my brother…" She'd been the one to find Charles. The one to hold his hand and beg him to live. He'd still been alive when she burst into his home office. Still been struggling to speak even as blood had dripped from his mouth. He'd been stabbed, again and again. Defensive wounds had been all over his arms, and his chest — there had just been so much blood. He should have been safe. Should have been protected. His home was secure — he had a state of the art security system. But someone had gotten past his safeguards.

A killer who'd never been caught.

"I'm sorry about Charles. You know he was my friend." Blane heaved out a hard breath. "Is that what this is about? You couldn't save Charles but that fellow out there, you think that because he survived the shooting it's some kind of sign or something?"

"It's a miracle he survived."

Blane shook his head. "No. I'll get a local doc to examine him. I'm thinking the EMT was just wrong about his injuries. No miracle."

He didn't understand. "You will call the Miami authorities, won't you?"

"Yes."

Some of the tension left her shoulders.

"And you *will* watch your ass with him?" Blane pressed right back at her. "He's a stranger, Shelly. You can't trust him. And you damn well can't keep the guy in your home."

***

Many hours later, John walked down Discovery's small main street, far too aware of Shelly at his side. He'd stayed at the sheriff's station, been grilled by Blane Gallows, been poked and prodded by an absolutely ancient local doctor. After the exam, the doctor had sworn that there was no way John could possibly have been shot the night before. After all, there were no signs of a recent injury on John's body.

"The sheriff doesn't want me near you." He stopped at the corner of the street, his gaze sweeping over the buildings. They were all nestled side by side, and bright, festive holiday lights decorated the exterior of the shops. Sunset was just sweeping over the mountains, but those lights were already shining brightly. Wreaths hung on the doors, and Christmas music played from nearby speakers. The snow had stopped falling, but a light coat of white dusted the town.

"Blane is suspicious of you." Shelly pulled her coat closer to her body. "He has cause, don't you think?"

She was shivering. He took off his coat — a
coat she'd bought him — and wrapped it around
her. Shelly had picked up far too many clothes
for him, and it had made him uncomfortable
when she paid for them. But he didn't have any
money. A man with no past — hell, he'd been so
happy to escape that he hadn't even thought
about how he'd survive in the world. He'd been
scraping by while he tracked down Shelly.
Picking up odd jobs, but he'd need more. He'd
need —

"Thank you," she gave him a quick smile as
she seemed to sink into his coat.

His heart warmed a bit. Her smile did
strange things to him. The wind blew and a lock
of her hair slid over her cheek. Without thinking,
his hand lifted and he brushed her hair back. But
then his fingers lingered against her cheek. They
were so close. She smelled so good. She was real,
not some dream, and he'd never wanted
anything more.

She didn't back away. He heard her breath
catch, and he felt her edge a bit closer to him. He
wanted to slip into her mind. To see what she
was thinking, to see if maybe, *maybe* she wanted
him, too. If she wanted a kiss. Something so
simple.

John was sure he'd kissed women before.
Sure he'd had lovers. But he didn't remember
them. And he wanted to know what a kiss with

Shelly — he wanted to know what that would feel like.

"I shouldn't…" Her voice was quiet. Husky. Sexy.

He started to back away from her.

But Shelly's hands rose. They pressed to his chest. "I shouldn't want you this way. This much. It's not quite normal, is it?"

Now he laughed. The sound was too rough. "What do I know about normal?"

"You're a stranger, and I should be afraid. Blane's right. I shouldn't trust you."

As far as John was concerned, Blane could go screw himself.

"But you touch me, and something happens." Her voice stroked over his skin. "My whole body tightens. And I yearn. I need."

Was the woman trying to bring him to his knees? "I want to kiss you."

She swallowed. "I know."

And she still wasn't backing away. The music was playing around them. Christmas lights were flickering behind her. The whole scene — it was so different from the life he'd known in that hell of a lab. It was like a dream.

No, she was the dream.

"I want to kiss you, too," Shelly confessed.

With those words, she sealed both of their fates.

"What could a kiss hurt?" Shelly asked as she rose onto her toes. "Just a kiss."

His hand slid under her chin, and his head lowered toward her. His whole body was tight as he put a stranglehold on his control. His lips pressed to hers. A soft, light kiss. Gentle. Sweet.

And then her lips parted. Her tongue slid against his lips.

And his control cracked.

Not just cracked — shattered.

He pulled her closer. Held her tighter. His tongue thrust into her mouth. He tasted her and felt drunk. Desperate. She gave a little moan in the back of her throat, and the sound made him wilder. His cock shoved against the front of his jeans, fully erect and eager — just from her kiss. He was kissing her harder, deeper, and he didn't want to stop. Desire had exploded within him, and he wanted so much more.

He lifted her up because he needed to be closer. He turned, holding her easily, and he caged her against the bricks of a nearby building. His mouth didn't leave hers. Her nails sank into his shoulders, and her body arched against him. They were on a street, people were around them, and he didn't care. He had what he wanted, and he wasn't going to let her go.

One kiss.

Yes, she'd sealed both their fates.

He wanted —

The whistle reached him. The fast, hard rush of air. The same sound that he'd heard on that damn mountain road. The whistle of wind that shouldn't be there.

A bullet. Coming for my Shelly.

He jerked her to the side, shoving them both to the ground.

"John! What—"

The bullet sank into the bricks above them, sending chunks raining down. He was on top of Shelly, shielding her with his body, so nothing hit her.

Another shot was fired. There was no crack of the gun deploying because the shooter was smart. Too fucking smart. This shot was closer, but it missed them, sinking into the bricks again.

People were nearby on the street. A mother and son holding hands. John realized they could walk straight into the line of fire.

"Stay down," he told Shelly. "*Down.*" Then he ran for the mother and son, grabbing them even as the mother screamed.

Another bullet whistled through the air, he could practically feel it—and it was coming for *him*. The shooter was aiming for *him*.

This time, he was the target, not Shelly.

He picked up the mother and her child, rushing them away from the open street and toward the side of the building even as he felt a burn across his shoulder.

People were screaming. Voices were rising.

He put the mother and child down next to Shelly. Shelly's eyes were wide, scared. "John? John, you're bleeding!"

He didn't hear the whistle of another bullet coming toward him. He looked back, judging the wind, trajectory...figuring out where the bastard must have been. *Close by.* "I'm getting him." Keeping his body low, John rushed away from her.

"John!" Shelly yelled.

The boy started crying.

"John!"

And he moved as fast as he could, knowing that he had to stop the bastard before anyone was hurt.

CHAPTER FIVE

"What's happening?" the woman beside Shelly cried, her voice breaking as she clutched her son tighter. The little boy appeared to be barely six years old. He had on a bright, Christmas sweater and his cheeks were a dark red. Tears spattered his cheeks.

Shelly patted his hand. "It's okay. You're safe."

"Who is shooting? It was a shot, wasn't it?" The mother clutched her son even tighter. "But I didn't hear the gunfire."

Shelly hadn't heard it, either. But her super soldier had. She wanted to rush after him, but, unlike John, she had no idea where the shooter was. And if she chased after John — would she just put them both in more danger? "It's going to be okay," Shelly promised. "My friend will keep us safe."

"If he doesn't get himself killed," the woman whispered back.

Shelly's gaze darted toward the street.

***

John burst onto the top floor of the old theater. The theater sat across the street from the spot he and Shelly had been just moments before — and he knew the theater had been the shooter's location. The door banged against the wall as he rushed inside, and the man waiting there spun around.

And he aimed his gun right at John.

"Freeze!" Sheriff Blane Gallows barked.

John didn't freeze. He rushed right at the sheriff and he knocked the gun out of the guy's grip. The handgun flew across the room even as John shoved the sheriff back against the nearby wall, holding him there with a tight grip on the man's neck.

Blane clawed at John's hand.

"Did you shoot at me?" John snarled. But…no, wait. The sheriff's gun was wrong. *Wrong weapon.* John glanced back around the room. The handgun was on the dirty floor. The upper floor of the theater was dusty, littered with old trash. Closed in. He inhaled, trying to pull in the scent of the shooter, but he just got Blane's scent. Blane's and —

"L-let the sheriff go!" A shaking voice demanded.

A young, redheaded deputy stood in the doorway. The same guy John had seen at the station. The fellow's bright red hair stuck out from his head at odd angles, and the gun trembled in his grasp. Another handgun, a Glock. Still not the right weapon. John knew the shooter had used a rifle. He'd seen the bullet that had lodged into the brick wall.

Blane kept clawing at his hand. Slowly, John let the guy go. Blane sucked in a desperate gulp of air. "Not...shooter..." Blane heaved. "F-figured out...was on...st-street..."

"You came up here looking for the guy," John realized, backing up. "Where in the hell is he?"

"G-get away from the sheriff!" the deputy's voice cracked on his order.

John whirled toward him. "Get your ass back down to the street. Make sure Shelly is okay. There are too many civilians down there. Let them know the shooter is gone."

Gone. Fucking *gone*. And John could only smell the dust and the stale scent of sweat in that place. Blane's sweat. The deputy's. But...

He hurried to a window—one that faced away from the street. *Not the one the bastard used to take his shot.* This window was still open, letting in cold air, and when he looked outside, John saw that an old ladder had been propped up against the back of the theater. Below in the snow that covered the ground, he could see the dark mark of footprints. Eyes narrowing, John heaved his body right through that window.

"Stop!" Blane yelled. "What the hell—"

But John was already through the window. He landed easily, his knees not even buckling, when he hit the ground. He glanced back up and saw Blane gaping down at him.

Without a word, John followed those prints. They circled around the building, and then disappeared on the sidewalk—the walk that had been swept clean of snow. John found himself in front of the theater, with cars rushing down the street. He looked to the left, to the right, and saw no sign of the bastard who'd been taking aim at him.

John's hands clenched into fists. Sonofabitch. *I will find you.*

***

"I still don't think it's a good idea for the guy to stay here with you," Blane groused to Shelly. "But you aren't listening to me, are you?"

They were back at Shelly's cabin. The jerk who'd taken a shot at them was in the wind, and the sheriff was trying to convince Shelly that she needed to kick John out onto the street.

John crossed his arms over his chest and waited near the fireplace. *Not happening, buddy. There's no way I'm leaving her.*

Shelly gave a soft sigh. "I hear you, Blane, but no, I'm not listening. John doesn't have any other place to go. I'm not turning him out after he's saved my life again and again."

Blane swore and glared at John. "I don't like you."

John inclined his head. *The feeling is mutual.*

Blane rubbed his neck. Bruises had appeared on his skin. Bruises in the shape of John's fingers. "I could arrest him for assault. The guy attacked me—"

"Because I thought you were the shooter." John didn't move from his post. "You were in the room above the theater, after all. And you pointed your gun at me."

"I was looking for the damn shooter!" Now Blane sounded outraged. "I wasn't the enemy."

John shrugged. "That's why I let you go."

Blane stalked toward him. Suspicion was heavy on the fellow's face. "You moved so fast when you attacked me. Barely even saw you— like you were a freaking blur. Then you jumped out of that window like it was nothing. Didn't even stumble from a *three-story drop*."

Once again, John shrugged.

"That shit isn't normal." Blane's gaze swept over him. "You're hiding secrets. Fair warning, I'm going to discover them. Every single one."

"Good luck with that." John swiped his hand over his jaw, scraping at the dark shadow that had grown there. "When you find those secrets, be sure to share them with me. I'd kinda like to know them myself."

The floor creaked as Shelly crept closer.

Blane leaned toward John. His voice dropped as the sheriff said, "Hurt her, and I'll bury you."

The sheriff didn't need to worry on that score. "Hurting Shelly is the last thing I'd ever do."

But Blane didn't look convinced.

"You should go now, Blane," Shelly urged him quietly. "It's getting late."

After another glare at John, Blane headed for the door. Shelly followed him, and John heard her promise that she'd call the sheriff if there was any trouble. While she locked the door, John bent and put fresh wood in the fireplace. He took a few moments to get the fire blazing, pushing at the wood and watching the flames flare as he crouched before the blaze.

He could feel Shelly behind him. She was a few feet away. Not close enough to touch. Not yet.

He'd tasted her before. He'd had her in his arms, and then some asshole had taken a shot at him.

"You have blood on your shirt."

He'd almost forgotten about that. "Bullet grazed my shoulder. It's nothing. Already healed."

"I can't quite get used to that. You being Superman and all."

He rose and turned toward her. The warmth of the fire was at his back. "I'm not Superman." But if he was, fuck, she'd damn well be his kryptonite. Did she get that? Did she understand that he'd do anything for her? That he went a bit crazy when she was in danger?

She rubbed her hands over the front of her jeans. "You saved my life again. You're making a habit of that."

"Not so sure he was aiming at you this time." Because that hit to his shoulder had been deliberate. "I think he wanted to take me out." John took a step toward her. He heard the growl of Blane's engine outside. "Smart move on his part. Because as long as I'm standing, I'm not going to let anyone hurt you."

Her head tilted as she stared up at him. John closed the last bit of distance between them. He wanted to touch her. Wanted it so badly that his hands clenched into fists so that he could control the temptation. She gazed back at him, and for a second, John could have sworn he saw yearning in her eyes. The same kind of stark, desperate yearning that he felt.

He leaned toward her —

"What if you have a family out there? Someone who is missing you right now?"

"John Smith didn't have a wife. You saw that in the obituary." His obituary. How warped was that?

"Doesn't mean you don't have a lover out there. Someone who is missing you. Someone who needs you."

"I was trapped in that hell for months." He'd tried hard to keep track of the days, but sometimes they'd all blurred together. "And I don't remember any other woman. Don't remember any lover. Only *you*."

"I still don't understand how. Why." Her lashes swept down to cover her gaze. "Do you think you saw me, in Miami? Because that's where I live. Perhaps our paths did cross, but how could I forget you?" Her lashes lifted. Her stare held his. "I don't think I could ever forget someone like you."

He didn't speak.

"Even though you knew the shooter was out there, you ran to save that mother and her son on the street. You might not remember who you were before you woke up in that lab," she gave him a quick smile, "but I think I'm learning a whole lot about the kind of man you were. The man you *are*. You risked your life to save strangers."

John shook his head. "I would have come back even if I'd taken a shot in the heart. We both know that."

She studied him a moment, then shook her head. "I don't think that thought ever entered your mind. You saw someone in danger, and you stepped up. You want to know who you were before? I can tell you. You were a good man." She gave a quick nod. "A brave man."

She didn't understand. Didn't know about the darkness he could so often feel inside of himself. A fury that grew to a chilling degree. A twisted hate that had festered for the scientists and doctors in that godforsaken lab. And earlier, when she'd been with Blane and the sheriff had been touching her, jealousy had burned within John. Dark emotions seemed to thrive within him. "I'm not so sure I am good."

Her smile stretched. "Then I'll have to prove to you that you are." Her fingers slid up his arm. Paused at his shoulder. "This is the second shirt that a bullet has ruined."

Two for two.

"Why don't you go ahead and shower off the blood? I'll get you a towel." She backed away.

Retreated.

He stood there, aware of the fire crackling behind him. He watched as she turned and headed toward the darkened hallway. "We aren't going to talk about it?"

She stilled. "It?"

"The kiss. The fact that I got one taste of you and nearly went mad because I wanted so much more. I still want more. I'm staring at you right now, and I want to touch you. Want to taste you."

She raised her hand, pressing it against the wall. "What if there's someone else out there for you?"

"There isn't." He was absolutely certain of that.

She glanced over her shoulder, her gaze finding his.

"There is only you." He knew that, deep in his bones.

But she looked away. "I-I'll get that towel." And she ran from him.

That was okay, though. They were alone in the cabin. Wasn't like he couldn't find her. Wasn't like she could escape.

***

Put down the towel and walk away.

Shelly paused outside of the guest bathroom. The door was slightly ajar, and tendrils of steam snaked into the hallway. Water thundered from inside, and she knew that John was already in the shower. She should just slide her hand inside, put the towel on the sink and hurry away.

That was absolutely what she should do.

And she would do it.

She rapped on the door and raised her voice. "John! I've got a towel. I'm just going to put it on the sink." She slipped her hand inside, fumbling around and then — then warm, strong fingers curled around her wrist.

The door had opened fully. More steam slid out, wrapping around her.

John was there. Clad only in the jeans that hung low on his hips. His face was cut into hard, determined lines, and his eyes glittered.

"Wanted to bring it to you — um, the towel, I mean." She tried tugging on her wrist. He didn't let her go. "I'll be in the den if you need me."

"I do."

He still hadn't let her go.

He *had* taken the towel and tossed it aside. His fingers slid along her inner wrist and the soft caress had her breath coming faster.

"I do need you, Shelly. You've been in more fantasies than I can count. I need you. I want you. Let's both be very clear about that."

Her heart was racing too fast.

Only…he let her go. "But you're still scared of me. And I *hate* that. I'll say it a thousand times, I'll never hurt you. You can trust me."

They'd just met. They'd —

"You say I'm a good man. You think I am. Baby, I can be so good to you. I can give you so much pleasure. Just give me the chance."

Oh, wow.

His hands fell to the snap of his jeans. "The shower is more than big enough for two."

Yes, yes it was. But...

If I cross this line...She was very much afraid of what would happen. Not afraid of him. Afraid of herself. Afraid of the way she'd absolutely lost control with his kiss. One kiss wasn't supposed to make her ignite that way. One kiss wasn't supposed to send her body flying into overdrive. One kiss wasn't supposed to make her go wild.

But it had.

He had.

She hurried out of the bathroom, pulling the door shut as she exited. Then she just stood in the hallway, trying to get her composure back. She wasn't used to men like John. Men who just said what they wanted. No games. Men who were so strong and dominant. The closest she'd come to someone like him...that had been Blane. And they'd sure crashed and burned as lovers.

Would she crash and burn with John? Even if she did, would the pleasure be worth it? Because judging by the way the man could kiss, she was sure he'd be one hell of a lover.

Her hand rose and pressed to the wood of the bathroom door. All she had to do was go inside.

There was no one there to judge. Just her. Just John.

She wanted him. He wanted her.

So why was she hesitating? Why not take the risk? Why not take him?

Get a grip, Shelly. She was running on adrenaline. That was it. Her emotions were out of control, and she just needed to calm the hell down. Shelly hurried away from the bathroom and returned to the den. She'd kicked off her shoes when she first arrived at the cabin, and now she sat on the rug before the fire, curling her bare feet beneath her.

She stared at the flames and she tried very, very hard to get her much needed grip.

***

He watched the cabin. Saw the lights shining from inside. Caught the scent of the smoke drifting on the breeze. Shelly Hampton was in that cabin. His target. But she wasn't alone.

That damn bastard was with her. The fool who *should* have been dead. The guy was getting in his way. Screwing things up.

He'd worked too long and too hard for screw-ups. His rifle was on the ground beside him, but it was useless right then. He didn't have a shot. He didn't see anyone near the windows. For all he knew, Shelly and the bastard were fucking somewhere in the cabin.

He reached into his boot. Pulled out a knife. The same knife he'd used on her brother. He'd never killed anyone with a knife before. Not until Charles Hampton. But it had been surprisingly easy. And it had felt…

Personal. Only fair, really. The kill *had* been personal. *Exactly what you fucking deserved.*

Maybe he'd use the knife on Shelly, too. Give her what she deserved.

But first, he'd have to get rid of her protection. The asshole who thought he could play hero.

Wrong move. The hero was going to get a swift trip straight to hell.

CHAPTER SIX

His hair was still wet when John strode into the den. He followed Shelly's sweet scent into the room and found her gazing at the fire. She looked so small curled on the rug, and her long hair trailed over her shoulders. He didn't think he'd made a sound, but she gave a little start and glanced back at him.

Her cheeks were a soft pink. Probably from the warmth of the fire. Her lips were red, full, and he couldn't stop thinking about how they'd felt beneath his mouth. She still wore her green sweater and the jeans that hugged her legs and hips so well.

She still made him ache.

"That was fast." She gave him one of her quick smiles. The smile that vanished so quickly it didn't have a chance to light her eyes. "I thought you'd stay in there longer."

"And I thought that if I did, you'd escape upstairs." He headed toward her. Hesitated, and stared down at her. He wore a fresh pair of jeans, and he knew they weren't doing much to hide his arousal. That was the thing — he pretty much just had to look at Shelly and he got turned on. "The cold water didn't help."

Her gaze dipped down his body then snapped back to his face. The red on her cheeks deepened. She jumped to her feet. "John—"

"Didn't expect it to help." But he'd needed to try something. "I can keep my hands off you, baby. You don't need to worry." His hands were at his sides even though he *did* want them on her. It was her call, though. Everything — her choice.

"I do worry." Her voice was low. Her gaze never left his. "Because I know what will happen if you do touch me. I was in here, staring at the fire, and thinking about exactly what would happen."

"You want me to leave." Hell, he *couldn't* leave her. He was sure she was in danger and—

"I've lost so many people that I care about this year. I've been on my own, just trying to put one foot in front of the other and survive." She rocked forward a bit. "I haven't been thinking about the future. I've been thinking about one moment at a time. It's how I've gotten through the days and nights."

"Shelly…"

"I don't know how I'm supposed to react to you. I don't think I'm supposed to feel this way."

"Maybe you don't need to think about what you're 'supposed' to do." His words were a rumble, too rough and hard. That was how he felt around her. Too rough. Too dangerous. She was silk and sensuality, and he was darkness. Trouble. Hell, what was he doing? He turned away from her.

But Shelly's hand flew out and curled around his arm. "I was always the good girl growing up. Never took any risks. Didn't fall for the bad guys that my big brother warned me about."

John rubbed his hand over his chest, aware of a sudden ache.

"Playing it safe didn't stop me from hurting." Her fingers slid up his arm and his eager cock jerked. Just from that little touch. "I guess we can get hurt no matter what we do."

His body was tight. "You should stop touching me."

"Why?"

He'd be blunt. "Because it makes me want to fuck you. And I don't think that's what you—"

"I'm ready for a risk."

John shook his head. She *hadn't* just said that.

"Life is short. I learned that lesson the hard way. Well," now she gave a quick, nervous laugh, "I guess it's short for anyone but you."

She was still touching him. Her fingers slid down his arm in a light caress.

"I stared into the fire, and I thought about having your hands all over me. I thought about what we could do together. I thought about risks.

I thought about tomorrow." She came closer, and she put her mouth on him. A light kiss that grazed his arm. "And I thought that I didn't care. I've never felt this way." She stared up at him. "Never wanted someone so much that I forget to be good."

She was saying that she wanted to be with him.

His hands had fisted. But her hand lowered, and her fingers closed around his right fist. Her touch was so soft. "Come upstairs with me," Shelly whispered.

Then she let him go. She strode toward the staircase, and his gaze dropped to her hips. Sexy as hell hips. She paused at the base of the stairs, her hand rising to rest against the banister. "That is…if you want to…"

Did he look like a fool? John bounded toward her, and he scooped Shelly up into his arms. If she wanted him, then she'd get everything that he had to give. He carried her up those stairs, practically running because he was so eager.

"The first door on the right," Shelly told him. "It's—"

He already knew which room was hers. Her sexy scent was stronger in there. He kicked open the door and carried her inside. He put her down near the bed, and John fought hard to *not* rip off her clothes.

Shelly smiled at him. Then her hands went to the hem of her sweater. She lifted it over her head and dropped it to the floor. Her breasts were covered by a silky, red bra. Sexy as fuck. Her hand went to the waist of her jeans, and she unhooked the button. Lowered the zipper. The jeans slid down her body, and his gaze locked on the matching red underwear that covered her sex. Barely a scrap.

He took a step back.

"John?" Now her voice was husky, hesitant.

He forced his teeth to unclench. "I'm worried...I'll be too...rough." Even his voice sounded like grating nails.

But Shelly just gave a light laugh and moved closer to him. "Rough isn't a problem. In the right circumstances..." Her fingers trailed over his chest, leaving a path of fire on his skin. "I think it can be sexy."

His heart was about to jump out of his chest, and his dick was rock hard. He wanted nothing more than to strip away the scrap of silk over her sex. To tear it away. To plunge into her.

Shelly didn't get it. Rough for him *was* dangerous. He had to control his strength at every single moment. Especially with her. He could *never* hurt her. And he had to make sure she enjoyed the sex between them. Not just enjoyed it—he needed her to crave him. To want him as badly as he did her.

Once wasn't going to be enough for him. He already knew that.

He needed her as lost and obsessed as he was.

"John…" Her fingers slid down his stomach, hovered over the top of his jeans. "You don't…if you don't remember your own name, if you don't remember anything before that lab…" She swiped her tongue over her lower lip, and he growled instinctively. *I want her mouth.* "Then do you remember having sex?"

He'd had fantasies…fantasies of her. Fantasies of them on the beach, of him stripping away her bikini.

"*Have* you had sex since you got out of the lab?"

"No." But he knew what sex was. And he knew what he wanted from Shelly.

She unbuttoned his jeans. "I can help you. I can show you anything you need to know." With a soft hiss, the zipper pulled down.

He wasn't wearing underwear, and his overeager cock shoved toward her hands. And when she stroked him, when her fingers curled around him, pumping him from root to head…*Fucking good.* His breath shuddered out.

She leaned forward and pressed a kiss to his chest. Then another. Light, soft kisses as she made her way to his nipple. And her tongue was sliding against him, flicking, tempting, even as her hands squeezed and pumped and pushed him — *too far*.

He picked her up. Dropped her on the bed.

"John —"

He grabbed the scrap of red around her hips. He meant to just pull the panties off her, but they tore, exposing her sex to him. Her bare, pretty pink sex. Her legs were splayed apart, but his hands closed around her thighs and he widened them even more.

The pounding of his heart echoed in his ears. He had what he wanted. Right there. He had her. And he was going to take her.

John put his mouth on her. Her hips heaved up, arching toward him, and his hands moved, fast, locking her in place, keeping her still beneath his mouth so that he could lick and kiss and taste. And the more he tasted, the wilder he grew. He'd looked for her, searched for her, hunted for her. She'd been in his head for so long.

But now she was beneath his mouth.

Now she was his.

"*John!*" His name burst from her, high-pitched, breaking with pleasure as she shuddered beneath him.

He looked up and saw that her eyes were wide, her cheeks flushed. She was so incredibly beautiful as she climaxed. As she came — for him.

He couldn't wait. He pulled back, started to put his cock at the entrance to her body —

"Protection," Shelly gasped out. "In...nightstand..."

He opened the nightstand. Found a box of condoms there.

"Picked them up..." She was still gasping. "While you were...getting clothes earlier...thought...just in-in case..."

He smiled at her. "Not just in case," he told her and he bent, pressing a kiss to her throat. "I'll *always* want you." He tore open the condom wrapper, but her soft fingers took it from him. She smoothed the condom over his dick, and he had to lock every muscle in his body so he could stay sane a little longer.

Explode in her. Take her. Take...

"There," Shelly whispered. "I don't want to wait any longer."

But she still had on her bra. And he had to see her breasts. Had to lick them. Kiss them. He slid his hand behind her back and jerked open the bra's clasp. Then he was shoving her bra out of the way. Her nipples were tight and dark pink, and he took one into his mouth even as he drove into her.

Drove so deep.

She cried out his name.

He kept licking her nipple. Sucking. Kissing. Growing rougher with every second that passed. She was so tight. Hot. His hands fisted in the bedding beneath her, yanking up the sheet and balling it in his fingers.

He thrust into her. Withdrew. Sank deep.

She climaxed around him. Shelly gave a quick scream as her body bucked beneath him, and her sex squeezed him with the contractions of her release.

He'd given her pleasure. Brought her to the brink. Pushed her beyond.

My turn. He let go. Became absolutely fierce. His mouth was on her body. Licking. Kissing. Marking her. He released the sheets. Grabbed her legs and pushed them over his shoulders so that he could have full access to her. So that he could have everything.

He wanted to mark her inside and out. He wanted her to mark him. He needed to brand this moment in his mind so that he could never forget it. So that no one could ever take it from him.

Never take her from me.

His climax hit him. The pleasure poured through his whole body as he stiffened. John held her tight, too tight, as the release burst from him. The pleasure seemed endless, wringing him out, blasting through every nerve and cell.

He stared into her eyes as he came. Saw the same wild pleasure in her gaze.

Slowly, so slowly, his heartbeat settled. He lowered her legs. Knew that he had to withdraw from her, but he didn't want to leave. He wanted to stay inside of her—hell, forever would be good.

But he worried he'd hurt her. John slid out of her body, moving carefully, and then he rose from the bed. He padded to her bathroom and ditched the condom. He looked around, grabbed a cloth for her, and warmed it beneath the water. When he came back into the bedroom, Shelly had pulled the covers up over herself. He hesitated. Maybe she wanted him to go.

He didn't exactly have a lot of knowledge about after-sex-etiquette, and for a moment, he floundered.

Take care of her.

He didn't have memories. He just had his instincts, and John's instincts pushed him across the room. He slid into bed beside her, slid his hands under the covers. Reached for her.

"John, wait, what are you—"

He carefully placed the warm cloth between her legs. "I'm sorry I was so rough."

Her breath hitched. "Told you...I don't mind."

"I was desperate for you. Desperation came make a man wild." He stared into her eyes. "I'll be more in control next time." He really hoped those words weren't a lie.

She didn't speak when he returned the cloth to the bathroom. Then he was back in the bedroom. And...

Maybe he was supposed to go downstairs. Go back to his guest room. Was that what a gentleman would do? He didn't know if he'd ever been a gentleman, but Shelly mattered to him, and he just didn't want to screw this up.

He turned for the door.

"You can stay, if you want."

Her words were low, but they still pierced right through him. He immediately headed toward the bed, and he eased beneath the covers with her. His body was stiff, and yeah, his eager dick was already twitching again. Just being near her turned him on, so that was nothing new.

Shelly moved toward him, and her fingers slid over his chest. "You might not remember having sex before, but I've got to tell you…you're really good at it."

John laughed. The sound escaped him before he realized it. Deep, a bit too hard but, it felt good. Being with her felt good. No, being with her felt right. "Sweetheart," he murmured as he picked up her hand and brought it to his mouth. His lips pressed to her knuckles. "You're fucking fantastic."

And she laughed, too. A soft chime that was absolutely beautiful. Her laugh made him feel warm. Made some of the darkness that clung to him ease a bit, and John realized…

This must be what it's like to be happy.

He hadn't been happy, not since he'd woken in that lab. He'd known pain, he'd known rage. But happiness? That had only come with Shelly.

She pressed closer to him. She *snuggled* against him. And he found himself putting his arm around her. She was warm and soft, and better than any dream he'd ever had.

"I don't do this," she whispered, and he could hear a faint slur in her husky words, as if she were just about to drift off to sleep.

"Do what?"

"Have sex with men that I've just met."

But I've known you for a long time. The thought pushed, unbidden, through his mind. She'd said they'd never met, but he knew her so well. "Why did you have sex with me?" John asked quietly.

Silence. Her breathing was easier, deeper, but he didn't think she'd slipped away to sleep, not yet. No, not just yet. "Shelly?"

"I wanted something good." Her breath brushed over his shoulder.

"Baby…" *I'm not good.*

"I saw how you saved that mom and her son…and you've saved me…" Her lips pressed to his shoulder. "I think you'd make a really good hero, and I could use one of those."

He sucked in a breath, but it felt cold in his lungs. He wasn't a hero. He was some kind of monster. Didn't she get that? He was a *dead* man who couldn't stay dead. A man with no past. But she'd let him into her bed. She'd let him into her body. And she was holding him as she slipped off to sleep. So trusting. So open.

His hold tightened on her. She was wrong about him, very wrong, but there was no way he could give her up. He needed her far too much.

***

"Watch her. Day and night. Do you understand me?"

John gazed out at the city below him. The lights were bright, shining in the darkness. The city was so fucking busy. Sometimes, he just wanted to escape the city. Escape his whole life. There was so much death and danger around him. Always had been.

"She doesn't make a move without you knowing, got it?"

He rolled back his shoulders. Felt the reassuring weight of his gun in the holster beneath his arm.

"This is the target."

He turned away from the window. John had a fast impression of a fancy office. Heavy, wooden furniture. Leather couch. Then he was staring at a photograph.

"Beautiful," he murmured. She was. All of that long, dark hair. Those gorgeous, fuck-me eyes. Deep and mysterious.

"Hunt her. Keep her in your sights at all times. And when it's time to act, I'll let you know."

He took the photo. "What's her name?" This new prey of his, who was she?

"Shelly. She's—"

***

John jerked upright, the images— memories?—fading from his mind. His breath heaved in and out of his lungs as he cast a quick glance at Shelly.

Still sleeping.

He slipped from the bed and rubbed a hard hand over his jaw. What in the hell had just happened? For a time there, he'd been back in some office, hearing some guy's voice so clearly, and then seeing Shelly's face.

Hunt her. Keep her in your sights at all times.

It had all been so clear. He paced to the window, pushing aside the curtains to stare into the darkness outside and then—

A faint flash of light. There one moment, gone the next, but that flash was all he needed to send his instincts into overdrive. He stared into the dark, and he let his senses rip wide open. He'd been trained at the lab—trained by the folks in the white coats to use his enhanced senses. They'd taught him how to tone down his senses when necessary so that all of the sounds and scents and smells didn't overwhelm him. But they'd also taught him how to use his newly acquired bonuses to his advantage.

He ramped up his power right then, and he heard…

The shuffle of steps.

Someone was out there. Watching the cabin. Watching *Shelly.*

Without any hesitation, John grabbed his jeans. He yanked them on and then he was running out of the bedroom, down the stairs, and bursting out of her front door. A light dusting of snow fell on him as he raced outside.

CHAPTER SEVEN

The cold woke her. Shelly's fingers slid across the pillow next to her, and she realized that John was gone. Her eyes opened as she sat up, pulling the covers with her. "John?"

The cabin felt…still. Quiet. Too quiet.

She glanced around the room, but saw no sign of him. Had he gone back down to his room? Maybe he'd been uncomfortable staying with her. She shouldn't have asked him, but she'd just felt so close to him. And she hadn't wanted that closeness to end.

She eased from the bed. Grabbed a terry cloth robe and wrapped it around her body. Shelly found herself creeping out of her room and tip-toeing down the stairs. The cabin's lower level was just as eerily silent as the upstairs area had been and when she glanced in John's room—empty.

A shiver slid over her body. "John?" Her voice cracked a little so she cleared her throat and tried again. "John?"

There was no answer. She headed toward the cabin's front door and her bare feet touched a bit of cold water. Water? *No, not water. Melted snow.*

Because John wasn't in the cabin. Her hand pressed to the wooden door as fear surged inside of her. He'd slipped away into the night.

***

He kept his body concealed as he hunted, and John made absolutely certain not to make a sound. He'd spotted his prey, caught him in the woods near Shelly's cabin. And he wasn't going to let the bastard escape. The fool wouldn't get off another shot. Not at him.

Not at her.

When he was close enough, John launched his body into the air. John hit his target, taking the guy down, slamming the fellow into the snow. He pinned the jerk beneath him, and John's fist rushed toward the SOB's face.

"Stop! Shit, it's *me!*" Sheriff Blane Gallows yelled.

His fist froze, but only for a moment. The sheriff's heart was racing in a triple-time rhythm, the guy's voice was cracking, and John could have sworn he smelled the man's fear. "You were in the theater. You were in the spot where the shooter took aim—"

He should have seen the truth then, John realized.

"I'm *not* the shooter!" Blane snarled at him. And he took a swing at John.

John dodged it, and he pounded his fist into Blane's face. Once, twice.

"Stop! That's — that's assaulting an officer!" Blane was trying to fight back, but the man was one weak-ass fighter.

John dragged the guy to his feet. Held him with one hand fisted in the sheriff's coat. John could see his prey perfectly in the night.

"You're not even wearing clothes," Blane snarled as blood dripped from his busted lip. "What in the hell is wrong with you?"

John was wearing clothes — jeans. He hadn't bothered with anything else because he hadn't wanted to let his prey get away. "You won't hurt Shelly." He'd kill the fellow first.

Blane's eyes doubled in size. "You really think *I'm* the bad guy here?" His fingers were creeping toward his holster.

In less time than it took to exhale, John had snatched the gun from Blane. He aimed it at the sheriff. "You're outside her cabin in the middle of the night. I saw your light from her bedroom window—"

"'Cause I was using my *phone* to check the time. I had the first shift, and I was looking to see when my relief would arrive." Blane had his hands up in the air, but his face was twisted with fury. "After everything that happened, I ordered a protection detail on Shelly. I wanted eyes on the cabin. Eyes on *her.* I wanted her safe, got it? That's why I'm out here. I'm not out here to hurt her. Shit, I love that girl."

John's hold on the gun tightened.

"I love her like *family*," Blane stressed. "So just calm your ass down, buddy. I'm here to keep her safe, not to hurt her. She's been hurt more than enough."

There was a heavy tension in Blane's words, and the sheriff's heart was still racing far too fast. John didn't take his gaze off the other man. "You should have told us that you were going to be watching the cabin."

Blane's chin notched into the air.

And John understood. "You didn't say anything because you don't trust me."

"Hell, *no,* I don't trust you. You come into town, and then Shelly is suddenly in danger. One plus one equals trouble, asshole." Blane lowered his hands. "And I got to say, I'm not even convinced Shelly *is* the target. Maybe this shooter — maybe he's after you, not her."

John kept the weapon locked on the sheriff. "Her brakes were sabotaged."

"No, the brakes were just worn. It was a rental car, and it didn't exactly have the best maintenance. Shit like that happens. It shouldn't,

but it does. This mystery shooter out there —
maybe he's gunning for you. Maybe it's been you
all along, and every moment that you stay with
Shelly, that's a moment that you're putting her in
danger."

No, no, that couldn't be true, could it? John
glanced back toward the cabin. He'd left Shelly
alone because he'd thought her attacker was in
the woods. "I need to get back to her."

"Asshole, you just *assaulted* a sheriff! The
only place you're going is jail."

John gave a low laugh. "I'd really like to see
you try and arrest me."

As if he'd been waiting for just those words,
Blane gave a snarl, and he lunged for John. But
John just stepped away — very, very quickly. So
quickly that he knew he'd look like a blur. Blane
missed him and slammed fast-first into the snow.

Blane spat snow from his mouth and lifted
his head. He stared at John with stunned eyes.
"What in the hell are you?"

John rolled back his shoulders. "I'm an
enemy you don't want." And he needed to get
back to Shelly. "You don't need to keep eyes on
the cabin. If anyone gets too close — the way you
did tonight — I'll know." He turned on his heel
and began heading back to the cabin.

"Humans can't move the way you do!" Blane
bellowed after him. "And I *know* you were shot
the first night with Shelly! I saw the pool of blood

on the ground. You shouldn't have been able to heal. You shouldn't have been walking around the next day like it was nothing."

John glanced back at the sheriff.

Blane was on his feet, glaring after him. "I'm asking again, *what* are you?"

"I'm the man who is going to stand between Shelly and any threat that is out there."

The sheriff brushed snow off his chest. "What if you are the threat to her? What then?"

John didn't answer the guy. He'd already been away from Shelly for too long.

"I'm coming after you!" Blane bellowed. "Your ass is going to jail! Do you hear me?"

Yeah, he heard the guy. But John took off, running back through the woods, rushing toward the cabin. His instincts were screaming at him. Telling him there was danger around him. But he couldn't locate anyone else in those woods. He didn't sense anyone else.

But trouble was close. Trouble was coming.

The cabin appeared before him. He bounded up the steps and just as he was about to pound on the door, it swung open. Shelly stood there, wearing a robe, her hair tousled around her shoulders.

"John? When I woke up and you were gone…" She grabbed him and pulled him into the cabin. "Why the hell were you gone? And why—" Her words cut off. "Why are you holding a gun?"

Because he'd taken the sheriff's gun. He put it on the table and kicked the door shut. Locked it.

"You don't have on a shirt." Shelly's voice rose. "Or shoes. And it's *freezing* out there. You need—"

"I just beat up your sheriff."

She blinked. "Say that again."

"I beat up the sheriff. He's probably making his way to his car, calling for back-up, and I'm pretty sure he's going to haul me off to jail for the rest of the night."

Her lips had parted in shock, but the shock only seemed to last a moment before she snapped her mouth shut and gave a hard, negative shake of her head.

"Yes." Blane wasn't just going to let this go. "He was watching your cabin. I thought he might be the shooter."

"It was just a mistake. You didn't know—"

"I punched him after I knew." *And* he'd taken the guy's gun.

Now her eyes were even wider. "John?"

His hand cupped her cheek. "A jail cell won't keep me away from you for long." Normal cells weren't designed to hold someone like him. The sheriff realized John was different. The sheriff was afraid of him. Good. Blane should be afraid.

"I'll talk to Blane," Shelly promised him. "I'll convince him to back off. We're old friends. He'll listen to me. He'll —"

"You care about him." And Blane had said he loved her.

"We're friends. Have been for a very long time."

In the distance, John could hear the growl of the sheriff's engine. He'd come to recognize that sound. The sheriff would be at their door soon. "I don't want to leave you unprotected. You can't stay at the cabin by yourself. Get Blane to put you in a safe house."

"You are *not* going to jail!"

He was. The growling engine was even closer. "Blane thinks that I might be the one putting you in danger. That it's my fault."

"What?"

"He thinks I'm the target, not you." And if the guy was right, then staying close to her put Shelly in the most danger. The sheriff's cruiser was right outside. Blane had come fast.

"No. This isn't happening."

John could hear the rush of footsteps, and then a fist pounded against the front door.

"Shelly!" Blane blasted. "Shelly, let me in!"

John's hand slipped away from her cheek. "You heard the man."

She didn't move. "And you'd better hear *me*." Her eyes gleamed up at him. "I'm not letting you get tossed in jail." Then she skirted around him and yanked open the door.

The light spilled onto Blane's furious face. His lip was swollen and still bleeding, and a bruise marked his jaw. He pointed to John. "You're under arrest, Smith."

Shelly caught Blane's hand, lowered it. "He thought you were a threat to me."

"Bullshit. He knew I was the sheriff. He knew *exactly* who he was attacking, *and* the jerk stole my gun!"

Shelly winced. She slid away from Blane, grabbed the gun, and offered it back to the sheriff. "Here. It's not stolen. It was…borrowed."

John crossed his arms over his chest. He wasn't going to lie. "I stole it. I don't trust the guy so I wasn't leaving him with a gun while my back was turned."

Blane bared his teeth at John. "And I don't trust you. You're the guy who is supposed to be dead. The guy who was supposed to have been shot in the back on that mountain road." He holstered his weapon. "You move too fast. Your reflexes are too good. You're too strong. You're some kind of supernatural freak, and I don't want you anywhere near Shelly."

Supernatural freak.

"Blane, stop it." Shelly's words were sharp. She strode to stand beside John. "We all need to calm down."

John slanted a glance at her. She looked small and vulnerable in her robe. And sexy as hell with her tousled hair and her red lips. She looked like a woman who'd just climbed out of bed and —

"Shit," Blane snarled. "You're screwing him."

John lunged forward.

"Stop!" Shelly grabbed him. Held tight. "This is *not* the way to avoid jail time. You can't keep attacking the sheriff."

He stilled, only because she'd asked him to stop. But he didn't like the furious twist of Blane's face.

"Shelly!" Blane snapped. "You don't know this guy! He's a stranger, and you took him into your bed?"

Her cheeks flushed. John heard the skip of her heartbeat.

She was embarrassed. Immediately, John stepped in front of her. "Watch yourself." His hands were already fisted as he faced off against the sheriff.

Warily, Blane glanced at John's hands. After a moment, his gaze rose once more. "Shelly, trusting the wrong man can be a fatal mistake."

Oh, hell, no. You just —

"Don't arrest him, Blane. Please." She was practically begging the guy. Shelly didn't need to beg anyone for anything. Not on John's watch. Not on —

"John's been through a lot, okay? There are things you don't know about him." She edged to John's side. "Things you don't understand."

She wasn't about to tell the sheriff about Lazarus, was she?

"I'm asking you as a friend," Shelly continued, "don't do this."

Blane's eyes blazed. "Shelly, the man is a threat. How can you not see that?"

John had heard enough. "I'd *never* be a threat to her."

"Your ass beat a *car* back to this cabin. You think that's normal shit? It's not. Nothing about you is normal, and I'm taking you in."

"Blane!" Shelly cried out. "*Don't.*"

Blane had cuffs in his hand. "I'm taking him in, Shelly."

John's back teeth clenched. "You'd leave her unprotected?" he gritted out the words.

Blane's face flushed. "Of course, not. I've got my deputy on the way out here now. He'll keep an eye on her for the rest of the night while you get comfortable in a cell at the station." His lips thinned. "You either faked your death in Miami, or you stole that poor guy's identity. And you just assaulted an officer. You're going in." His gaze cut to Shelly. "Don't keep looking at me like that. I'm doing this *because* we're friends. I want you to be safe."

While Blane's cheeks had flushed, Shelly's had gone pale. "If you do this, you know I'll just call my family's lawyer. I'll have John out by dawn."

"You do what you have to do." Blane moved toward John. "And I'll do what *I* have to do."

One punch, and John knew he could knock the guy out. But, then what? Shelly wouldn't run away with him. Not if he knocked out the sheriff right in front of her. Not if he let his rage out and he attacked.

Shit. *Shit.* The sheriff had backed him into a corner.

"You gonna fight me?" Blane asked him.

He wanted to but… "You swear you're gonna keep her safe?"

"You're the threat. My gut says the shooter is after you, not her. So if I remove you from her life…"

Then the sheriff thought Shelly would be safe. John lifted his hands. He'd play this game, for now. "You'd damn well better make sure a deputy stays with her every moment."

"I'm *coming* to the station," Shelly threw right back. "I'm not going to just stay here while you get tossed in a cell." Her hand squeezed his arm. "I'll go get dressed. I'll be right back just — *I'm not going to give up on you.*"

She rushed up the stairs. And he watched her, every single step of the way.

"Her heart is too soft," Blane's disgusted voice groused. "Always has been. She thinks you need help. She doesn't see you for what you are." He grabbed John's arm and led him to the door.

The snow brushed against John's face as he stepped outside. He inhaled and…

A bitter, acidic scent burned his nose. Frowning, his head turned toward the sheriff's vehicle.

"I'm expecting a call from the Miami authorities first thing in the morning. Gonna get some answers. And after your little stunt tonight, there's no way I'm leaving you out here with her." Blane pushed John toward the car.

John went forward, but only because he wanted to get closer to that vehicle. And with every step, the acidic odor grew stronger. "Someone messed with your brakes, too."

"What?"

John lifted his bound hands. "I can smell brake fluid. Bend down, get beneath your car, and you'll smell it, too. You've got brake fluid leaking out." The same trick that had been used on Shelly. "Bet you wouldn't make it down to the station before you lost control."

"You're talking bullshit!" But John saw that Blane's nose was twitching. The guy grabbed a flashlight from his vehicle. He shined the light in John's eyes. "Step your ass back, got it?"

John took a step back.

Blane crouched on the ground, shining the light under the car. "What. The. Fuck?" Not so much a question as an exclamation of fury. Blane jumped back to his feet. The light hit John once more. "How the hell did you know that?"

"I've got a good sense of smell." He paused. "You saw the brake fluid, didn't you? Spilling out all over the place."

"The brakes were a little funny on the way to the cabin," Blane muttered. "I didn't even think…" He jerked his hand through his hair. "No way is that a coincidence. Shelly's vehicle *and* mine?"

Shelly's feet rushed over the porch. "I don't want you taking him, Blane!"

John glanced back at her. She'd dressed in jeans and boots, and a big, black sweater.

"Don't worry." Blane's hands were on his hips as he glared at his car. "None of us are leaving in that ride."

She staggered to a stop at John's side.

Blane glared at John. "Did you just save my ass?"

John held up the cuffs, and with one hard tug, he broke them apart. "You're welcome."

CHAPTER EIGHT

"I can't stay in this cabin forever." Shelly paced in front of the fireplace. "I'm going stir-crazy. We've been inside all day long."

John sprawled on the couch. She could feel his eyes on her. It had been close to three a.m. before Blane and his deputies left her property. After he'd left, she hadn't exactly gotten a lot of sleep. She'd tossed and turned for hours, finally drifting off just before dawn. Nightmares had haunted the brief sleep she'd gotten.

Blane had told her that she needed to stay out of sight while his men kept patrolling the area. She kept waiting to get the all-clear from him, but so far, no such call had come. The day was nearly gone now, with deep shadows sliding across the mountain as sunset crept closer.

"What do you want to do?"

John's voice was so low and deep, and it cut right through her. They hadn't talked about the sex. The incredible, mind-numbing sex. They'd been too distracted by John's near arrest and the fact that someone had sabotaged Blane's brakes.

She'd been nervous around John all day long, too jumpy. So when he asked her what she wanted to do...in that voice that was pure sex appeal...

You. I'd like to do you.

"Your heart rate just kicked up," John noted quietly.

She put her hand over her heart. "What?"

His head tilted as he stared at her. "I can hear it. It's beating so much faster now. Are you scared?"

No, not scared. Or at least, she hadn't been, not until he'd said he could *hear* her heart beating.

"And your breathing is faster." He rose from the couch. Stalked toward her. "What's wrong?"

"S-someone is playing dangerous games," she stumbled over her words. "And I'm trapped here with a super soldier who can hear my heart beating. I think I might be entitled to a little freak out, don't you?"

His lips thinned. "I brought danger to you."

"No, you *saved* – "

"Blane thinks I'm the target. Not you."

Blane. Not Sheriff Blane, not anymore. One fist fight, and now they seemed to be besties.

"I'm the one with the screwed-up past. The lab I was in, baby, I only got out because someone blew it to hell and back. I'm an experiment, a freak – "

"*Don't!*" She didn't want him talking that way about himself, not ever.

"Maybe I was supposed to stay dead when that lab exploded. But you know me…" His lips hitched into a humorless smile. "Staying dead isn't easy for me."

And she was very glad for that particular fact. She grabbed his shirt-front and held tight. "Don't joke."

"I'm not." There was no humor in his eyes. "I've been considering this all day. I think Blane is right. I think I'm the target. I had it in my head that you were in danger. That I had to find you, but all I did was *bring* the danger to you."

She didn't like the hard note in his voice. Or the way that his expression seemed so cold. "John?"

"I thought by staying that I'd keep you safe. But I'm wondering if you would be far better without me. If I leave, I can lure the attacker away, I can stop him, I can—"

"Put a big, giant target on your back? No, dammit, *no*."

"The shooter is after me."

She shook her head, hard. "You don't know that. My family…my dad, he was really wealthy, okay? Very, very wealthy. He invented all kinds of things and made a million-dollar business. When he died, the money went to me and my brother." Her words were tumbling out. "But my brother was killed this year. Stabbed in his house. And now there's just me. What if…what if I *am* the target? I swear…" Now she walked away from him. Stood in front of the fire. Stared at the flames as her arms wrapped around her stomach. "I used to think someone was watching me," she whispered.

"Shelly…"

"Back in Miami. I promise, I could almost feel him." She licked dry lips. "I told my brother about it, and he confessed that we had enemies. Said he'd done a few deals that he shouldn't have taken. But he told me, Charles *promised* me that he'd take care of things. That he'd eliminate any threats." A tear slid down her cheek. "Two days later, Charles was dead. I was alone, and my whole life felt wrecked."

The floor creaked behind her. "What kind of deals did your brother take?"

She rocked forward onto the balls of her feet. "I don't even know. I wasn't involved in the business. I never wanted to be. My dad and Charles loved the work. The pressure. I didn't want to be involved in that world." She stared into the fire. "I—"

"You paint. You sketch. You spend hours getting lost with your work."

Yes, she did. Frowning, she glanced over her shoulder at him. "I didn't realize you'd gone down to my studio." Her studio was on the basement level of the house, and she hadn't gone in it, hadn't been able to open the door because since her brother's death, she'd felt so dead inside, too. Charles had been her confidant. Her constant. Without him, she'd lost so much of her joy in life.

Her main studio was in Miami, but Charles had put one in the cabin for her, too. She'd often become inspired in the mountains. She'd get lost with her work. *No, I used to get lost.*

John's brow furrowed. "Your studio?"

"The one downstairs. I—"

"I haven't been in your studio. The first night, you told me not to go down to the next level of the cabin, and I haven't."

Goosebumps rose on her arms.

"I've…seen you paint." His words were halting. "Seen you in a room with soft blue walls, with easels spread all around you. Your hair is in a ponytail and you wear paint-stained jeans."

Her goosebumps got worse.

"You paint late into the night, and when you leave the little studio, you aren't safe enough. You go out onto the street, not even looking around you as you hurry to find a cab."

Silence. She wasn't sure what she was supposed to say. The studio he was describing— it was her place in Miami. She'd painted the walls blue to match the ocean.

"I've scared you."

Yes, he had. "Is my heart racing too fast again?"

"I can see the fear on your face." His words held no emotion. "I think…I think I was hired to watch you."

Now she turned to fully face him. "Run that by me again."

He scraped a hand over the stubble on his jaw. "I had a memory. At least, I think that's what it was. While you were sleeping last night, when we were in bed together, this vision slipped into my head. I was in an office, some guy in a suit was hiring me, telling me to watch you. He gave me your picture."

Her heart wasn't just racing. It was about to burst right out of her chest. "Describe the man to me."

"About my height. Dark hair. Brown eyes. Nose was a little hawkish, looked like it might have been broken once before. He had a cleft in his chin—"

Her eyes closed and things started to make a whole lot more sense to her. "His nose was broken because he got into a fight when he was fifteen. Some jerks were making fun of his little sister, so he challenged them all after school. Took on four boys for her." She swallowed the lump that had risen in her throat.

"Shelly?"

She didn't speak as she turned away from him. When she'd called and asked Sammy to get the cabin ready for her, she'd given him a few special instructions. The very *first* thing she'd asked him to do was remove all the family photos. She just hadn't been up to looking at them. Not ready to see what she'd lost. So she'd had Sammy put those photos in her studio. She'd known she wasn't ready to paint. So the studio had seemed like a safe place.

She hurried down the stairs that would take her to the basement level of the cabin. The key to the studio hung on a blue ribbon next to the shut door. She took that ribbon even as she heard John following behind her. She slid the key into the lock and swung the door open.

Easels filled the room. Paint stained the floor. Huge windows looked out at the mountains. Because the cabin had been built on the edge of the mountain, the basement level still had a killer view. She loved that view—being able to stare straight into the sunset. But she wasn't looking at the view right then. Instead, she headed for the big, old fashioned trunk that sat near the back wall. She opened the trunk and saw the framed photos inside.

The very top photo was of her and her brother. They were surrounded by snow. Last Christmas. They'd come to the cabin. Even made a snowman as they laughed and just enjoyed being away from everyone and everything else. Her heart ached at the sight of the photo. Charles had such a big grin on his face. His cheeks were red from the cold and the photographer — Blane — had caught him mid-laugh.

"Is this the man...the man in your vision who hired you?" She turned the photo toward a quiet John.

His fingers brushed over hers as he took the frame. "Yes."

The ache in her chest just got worse. "My brother — he hired you." Puzzle pieces slipped into place for her. "He was worried about some business deals. Always so overprotective." A tear slid down her cheek. "He must have gotten you to be my bodyguard. He tried to tell me a few times that I needed one, but I just blew him off." A weak laugh spilled from her. "Big brother to the rescue again. He hired you and didn't tell me, and that's why you have memories of me. I must have been your last big case in Miami before — before..."

"Before I was stabbed and left to die?"

Her breath rushed out. "My brother was stabbed, too." Her gaze met John's. "You were working for him. It seems like a pretty big coincidence that you *both* were attacked that way."

His head inclined. "Yes, it does."

"The day you died…" Her eyes widened because she remembered that date. Remembered skimming the obituary for John Smith. Remembered the pang she'd felt. She hadn't said anything at the time because she'd wanted to focus on him, not her past. Not her pain. "Oh, my God. It was the day after my brother was killed."

"Shelly…"

"It *has* to be related." Everything was related. Everything was sliding into place. "That's probably even how you knew to come to Discovery in order to find me." Her gaze searched his. "Somewhere in your mind, you must have remembered this cabin. Charles probably told you about it. *That's* how you wound up in Discovery."

His expression had shut down.

"The attacks here…my God, maybe they are aimed at you." Her words were spilling out far too fast. "Because maybe…maybe you saw something down in Miami." Hope had her rising onto her toes. "Maybe you saw the man who killed my brother."

He put the photo down on a nearby table. He stared at it a moment, then his gaze slanted back to her. "You think the man who killed your brother is after me now."

She tried to choose her words carefully. "My brother was stabbed. *You* were stabbed a day later." Her voice was too high. "What if the same man attacked you both in Miami? And that same guy is after you now?"

His gaze hardened. "I don't remember anything about that attack."

"Not yet, but you said you just remembered the meeting with my brother, right?" She caught his hands and held tight. "It's possible more memories will return for you. You might remember who stabbed you that night in Miami. And even if you don't, *he* doesn't know that." He—the killer.

But John didn't look convinced. "Shelly..."

"Please, help me." She was not above begging. "I tried to find out who killed my brother in Miami, I worked with his partner for weeks, but we couldn't turn over anything. If you know, if that man is here, then we can stop him. We can do this."

His eyelashes flickered. "His partner?"

"After my dad died, Charles brought in a partner to help revamp the business. Devin Donley." And a wide smile split her face. "Of *course*! If you were working as a bodyguard, then Devin would know about it! I can call him, and he can come meet you. He's in Atlanta now for the holidays. It won't take him long to get here." She squeezed John's hands tighter. "Devin and Charles didn't have secrets. He'll know you. He'll know about your past."

"Shelly…" Her name came out as a growl, but she could see the hope finally flickering in his eyes.

"I'll call him," she said. "Just let me make the call. Let's see what happens."

John nodded.

She threw her arms around him. "We're figuring this out," Shelly whispered.

His hands closed around her hips. He lifted her up against him, held her tightly. So tightly. The warmth of his body pressed against her. For an instant, she remembered what it was like be skin to skin with him. To have his body covering hers. To feel the hard thrust of his cock into her.

He held her up with his easy strength, and her feet dangled over the floor. Her hands were on his shoulders, and their eyes were just a few inches apart.

"My past…" His voice was so deep and rumbling. "It won't change what's happening between us."

The words sounded like a warning.

"I want you. You want me. There's no going back from that."

No, there wasn't. "I should make the call."

His lips pressed together. He lowered her back to the floor, and she hurried toward the door.

"You're pretending it didn't happen."

Her hand rose, and her fingers curled around the doorframe. "No, I'm not." She didn't look at him. "I can still feel you against my skin. Still remember what it felt like when your mouth was on me." Her voice broke a bit. "I've never had a lover like you before." Someone who'd possessed her so completely. Someone who'd seemed to mark her very soul. She wanted to ask if sex was always that intense with him but...

He wouldn't know. He wouldn't know if the intensity they'd shared was just typical for him and his lovers. Or if it had been something special.

For her, it had been special. And that scared her.

"I should call Devin before it gets any later." She still wasn't looking back at him. "This is what you need, John. This is what you wanted. The key to your past."

She hurried back up the stairs, but his low words followed her.

"No, baby, you're what I need."

***

Blane read the Miami-Dade ME's report—he read the thing three times. The medical examiner had faxed the report to Blane's station.

According to the report, John Smith had been stabbed multiple times and left to bleed out in a dirty Miami alley. There'd been no evidence left behind. Nothing unusual discovered during the ME's exam.

"No next of kin," Blane muttered as he flipped through the papers. His eyes narrowed. "John's former commanding officer claimed the body." And the records didn't indicate exactly *when* the body had been claimed. Just that it had been.

Blane had checked and double-checked the fingerprints. The guy currently staying with Shelly *was* the same man who'd been stabbed in Miami. The same man who should have been dead and buried. Only he wasn't.

And he was a guy who had fucking super speed, super strength, and from what Blane could tell…super senses.

"Sir?" A light rap sounded from nearby.

Blane's head lifted up. His door was open, and his newest deputy, Nolan Hoover, stood in the doorway. Nolan's fist was still against the wooden doorframe, and his red hair shot out from his head at stiff angles.

"Sir, do you want to go over the schedule for the patrols at Ms. Shelly's place?" Nolan asked quietly.

Blane's eyes narrowed. He had an active shooter in his town. A freaking nightmare with the holiday season and all of the tourists in

Discovery. He needed this nightmare to end, and he needed it to end *now.*

***

"John Smith?" Devin Donley repeated the name. Static crackled over the line. "He's dead."

Shelly hunched her shoulders as she curled her fingers around her phone a bit more. "You know him, though, right? He worked for my brother."

"I know him." Devin's voice was measured. "But the guy is a dead man."

"He isn't." She was staring at the dead man. "He survived the attack in Miami. He's here with me right now."

Silence.

Had she lost the connection? Dammit, her phone was always going out in the mountains. "Devin?"

"Say it again, Shelly. Very, very slowly."

She blinked. "I said John Smith survived. He's here with me right now."

"Get the hell away from him."

What?

"Is he in the room with you?"

He was. He was less than five feet from her, and Shelly knew he could hear every single word that Devin spoke.

"The man is dangerous. The federal government is looking for him right now. Jesus, Shelly, you have to get away from him."

"The federal government? What are you talking about?"

"I had FBI agents come to my place in Atlanta just a few days ago! Guys in dark suits who made me nervous as hell. Didn't understand why they were asking about a dead man but, shit, guess he's not dead, is he?"

"No." She swallowed the lump in her throat. "He's not."

"You're at the family place in Discovery? That's where you are?"

"At the cabin. I wanted you to talk to John, to tell him about his past—"

"The man is a fucking ice-cold killer, that's what he is. I told your brother it was a mistake to hire him, especially to tail you. Guy got obsessed."

No, no, this wasn't right. It couldn't be right.

"Look, you're still friends with the sheriff, aren't you? Get to him. I'm leaving now. I'm still in Atlanta so it's going to take me a little while to reach you…"

John was stalking toward her. His face looked even harder, even more dangerous than it normally did.

"Get away from him," Devin blasted in her ear. "*Trust* me on this, the guy is trouble, he's—"

John took the phone from her. He swiped his finger over the screen, turning on the speaker. "I'd never hurt her."

Static crackled. *"John?"* Devin's voice seemed strangled.

"Shelly is safe with me."

"Don't you touch her!" Devin was practically screaming. "Your prints were all over Charles's home—I suspected you all along. Faking your damn death—I should have suspected something like this. You faked it so you couldn't be charged with Charles's murder!"

Shelly shook her head. No, *no.*

"Stay away from her!" Devin snapped.

"I'd never hurt her," John said again, voice roughening.

"I'm coming. Shelly, do you hear me? I'm coming to Discovery. Get away from that bastard. Get to the sheriff, now!"

The line went dead.

CHAPTER NINE

She was terrified.

Fear rolled off Shelly in waves. Her heart was beating far too fast, her body was trembling and…

"Breathe, baby," John whispered.

Her breath left her in a hard rush.

His hand rose, and she took a step back. Her retreat pierced John right in the heart. "I was just giving your phone back to you." His voice was quiet, without emotion. Mostly because he had put a stranglehold on his emotions. Rage and fear pounded through him — rage at the man named Devin who'd just wrecked the bond John had tried so hard to form with Shelly. And fear — gnawing, twisting fear because John was afraid that he wouldn't be able to convince Shelly to trust him again. "Go ahead," he urged when she made no move to take the phone. "Call the sheriff. Get him out here."

Her gaze dropped to the phone. No spots of color stained her cheeks. In fact, she was far too pale. Her trembling fingers reached for the phone.

He expected her to immediately call the sheriff. Instead, her hand fisted around the phone and her eyes — fearful but also angry, so angry — rose to his. "Have you been playing me all along?" He'd never heard that tone in her voice before. The cut of rage. The rasp of betrayal.

John shook his head. "I wouldn't —"

"I must have seemed so stupid to you." She took another step back. "Buying that whole story about you not having a memory. About you waking up in some kind of *lab*."

He wanted to take her into his arms. To hold her tight. "It's not a story. It's the truth."

"Is it?" She shook her head. "I've known Devin for over five years. He was my brother's best friend even before they became business partners. Hell, that's *why* they became partners. Charles wanted someone he could trust to help him run the company after my dad died. And Devin just told me that you were a threat."

"I'm *not*."

She retreated another step. His gaze slid over her shoulder and toward the front door of the cabin. Was she planning to run out? He couldn't just let her run away. It wasn't safe out there. The shooter — the attacker who'd been stalking her — he could be lying in wait. "Call the sheriff," John urged her.

"*Do* you remember your past? And tell me the truth!"

His lips pressed together. His past…

Waking up strapped to an exam table. Men and women in white lab coats, whispering. Whispers that he'd heard so clearly.

"He's back!"

"Another successful experiment."

"Will he be as strong as the others?"

"John!" Shelly cried out. He blinked. For a moment, he'd slipped away in his mind. "Talk to me! Tell me the truth."

"I only remember pieces of my past. Flashes." He kept his hands loose at his sides, kept his body relaxed. He didn't want her to see him as a threat. "Flashes of you."

Her chin lifted. "Because you were hired to watch me."

"Yes, I think so." His temples began to pound. She was too pale. He wanted to slip into her mind, to see what she was thinking, to see if any part of her still trusted him.

"Did you kill my brother?" The question seemed torn from her.

And, fuck, he couldn't lie to her. "I don't know."

Tears welled in her eyes, but she blinked them away. Staring straight at him, she slid her fingers over the screen of the phone. Then she put the phone to her ear. "Blane," Shelly whispered a moment later. "I'm coming to town. I know you still have a deputy watching the house. Let him know that I'm leaving."

"Is everything all right?" Alarm sharpened the sheriff's words.

Shelly was still staring straight at John. "I don't think so."

John stepped toward her. He had to do it. "Come and get her," he barked to the sheriff, knowing he was close enough that Blane would be able to hear his words. "Don't let her drive alone. Come and get her."

Her lower lip trembled. "I'm coming to town, Blane. I'll see you soon." She ended the call and held her phone tightly in one hand. Shelly still didn't look away from John. "I want to trust you. I look at you, and I swear, I feel this...this connection. Like there is something pulling me toward you."

"Shelly, you *can* trust me."

Her hair slid over her shoulders as she shook her head. "You just told me that you don't even know if you killed my brother. How do *you* know I can trust you?"

"Because you are my life." Truth. Stark. "When I woke in that lab, when those bastards in the lab coats killed me again and again, *you* got me through those days. They told me that my past was gone. Dead and buried, the way I should have been. But it wasn't. *You* remained.

You slipped into my head. Appeared in my dreams. You gave me hope. You made me believe that I was more than just some freak who'd been locked away from the world. You were out there, and I just had to survive long enough to find you."

The tears she'd tried to blink away before were back. One slid down her cheek. He had to touch her. *Had* to do it. John closed the distance between them, and Shelly stiffened. She didn't back away, though, and when his hand lifted to her cheek, when his index finger caught her tear, she didn't flinch away from him. Her eyes slipped closed. He bent and pressed a kiss to her cheek. "I found you," John rasped. He'd found her, and he'd give his life — over and over again — to keep her safe.

"John..."

"I don't know what kind of man I was before I woke up in that lab." His voice was too rough. "I just know who I am now. And right now, I fucking live for you. I would do *anything* for you. You don't have to worry about me hurting you because, baby, I never would." But everything had to be her choice. Everything.

So he stepped back.

She still gripped her phone. Her eyes were wide and dark. "You're so beautiful," he murmured. "Have I told you that?"

She looked over her shoulder at the door.

"I can walk you out, baby," he told her. *Don't run, let me walk with you.* "I can make sure there is no threat out there. I'd hear a threat coming, you know that. I didn't feed you a bullshit story. Everything about Lazarus, everything about me and the powers I have—all of that is true. Let me protect you."

"Even though I'm running *from* you?"

Dammit. "Yes."

She bit her lower lip. "I don't know what to do."

Trust me. He didn't say those words. Instead... "Let's go to town. Both of us. Let's go see the sheriff. Let's wait for this Devin fellow to arrive. We can figure out everything together. Or..." He rolled back his shoulders. "You can go alone." He didn't like that idea. Not one bit. What if the shooter tried to get her while Shelly was alone in the car? "You can go to the sheriff's station, but at least get the deputy to drive you." The guy who was out there, keeping an eye on the cabin. "I'll stay here. I can—"

Her left hand caught his. Such a soft, silken touch. "I let you make love to me because I trusted you."

Make love. Is that how she'd seen it?

"You saved those people in town. The mom and her son. You saved *me.* And when I look at you, I see a good man."

Only Devin had told her that he was a monster.

"We'll go to town together." She nodded briskly, as if she'd just made the decision. A done deal. "We'll talk to Devin together. We'll figure this out. If my brother hired you, if he asked you to look out for me, then that means Charles trusted you. He wouldn't have hired someone that he thought was a monster. Charles had good instincts about people." She let out a slow breath. "So let's get out of here. Let's go to town. Together."

He nodded. Damn, but she was something. Beautiful, sexy, and she was *trusting* him. Did she realize what a gift that was? How incredibly grateful he was to her?

"I'll get some shoes and my bag," she said. "I'll be right back." Shelly brushed past him and headed up the stairs.

He stood there a moment, feeling the tension ease from his body. She was giving him a chance to prove himself. And he *would* do it.

I wish I could fucking remember.

John stalked toward the front door. Before they left, he wanted to make sure the perimeter was secure. He flipped the locks and a few moments later, he was striding outside. The mountain seemed so still and quiet. The sun had vanished, and darkness swept across the mountain. The snow crunched beneath his feet as he walked.

He turned in a slow circle, letting his gaze sweep around the area. He didn't see anything suspicious. Didn't hear anything that set off his alarm bells. He strode around the cabin, making his way toward the garage. He wanted to take a look at the SUV before Shelly got into the vehicle, just to be on the safe side. He didn't smell anything suspicious in the air, but he wasn't going to take a chance with her. He unlocked the side door to the garage, slipped inside...

And a faint click reached his ears.

Just a click. Such a soft sound.

But it was a sound that didn't belong.

John whirled around, his gaze sweeping over the garage.

And then the place exploded.

***

Shelly was on the stairs when she heard the explosion. It boomed like thunder, and she could have sworn that she felt the whole cabin shake. "John? *John!*" Shelly raced down the stairs and scrambled outside. She almost fell on the icy ground, but then she was shuddering to a stunned stop as she stared at the blazing remains of her garage. About twenty feet away from the cabin, the old garage was a mass of flames. It had once been a workshop for her father, a place for him to tinker for hours. And now…

"John?" Shelly whispered.

The flames shot into the sky. Red and orange. Swirling. Scaring the hell out of her. Black smoke billowed in the air.

"John!" Now she was screaming his name, but John wasn't answering her. She didn't see him anywhere, and she knew, she *knew* he'd been in that garage.

Shelly rushed toward the flames, slipping and sliding across the snow. The smoke battered at her, and the heat from the flames lanced her skin. She coughed, choking on the thick, dark smoke. Chunks of the burning garage littered the ground. The fire was so hot, and in her mind, she saw John trapped in the wreckage of the garage, burning.

Even he couldn't come back from death if he was burned alive. Could he?

She didn't hesitate. Shelly yanked up her sweater to cover her mouth, and she ran into what was left of the garage. Tears streamed from her eyes as she dropped to her knees, trying to find better air, trying to crawl through that hell and find—

Her left hand touched him. She'd thrown her hand out, groping wildly, and her fingers hit his arm. She dropped the sweater she'd used to cover her mouth and both of her hands grabbed him.

"*John!*" Her scream came out as a wrenching gasp.

He wasn't moving. Blood trickled from his mouth. From his forehead. Burning boards were over his legs and she could see the ravaged skin of his arms. *Covered in blisters.* "I'm getting you out," she whispered. She kicked at the boards on his legs, making sparks fly and flames dance. She kicked and kicked until he was free. Shelly grabbed his arms as the fire raged, and she hauled him back, dragging him across the floor as she pulled with all of her might. She fell twice. Felt the rush of flames all around her, but Shelly didn't give up. She kept dragging him, dragging and dragging until she hit the ground — only this time, she fell into the icy safety of snow.

A wild laugh escaped her. They'd gotten out. A loud, terrible groaning filled the air, and she watched, her eyes still streaming from the smoke and the flames, as the roof of her garage collapsed.

The deputy who'd been assigned to watch her house — Shelly knew he should be arriving any moment. He would have seen the flames. He would have called for back-up. She crawled closer to John. "You just need to hang on," she said to him, but her voice was a croak, weak from the smoke and fire. "You're okay." Her hands smoothed over John's face. Down his neck. Over his chest.

And she realized that he wasn't okay. Because John wasn't breathing.

Her own breath left her in a whoosh. "John?" She pushed her hands against his chest. "Come back. Come back right now. Do you hear me? *Come back –* "

"Aw, Shelly, sorry, sweetheart, but the dead don't come back."

She stiffened at that voice, the low, amused rumble that had come from right behind her. A rumble that was familiar to her because she knew the speaker. She'd known him for years. He was a friend, almost like family. So close. Slowly, her head turned.

And her brother's partner, Devin Donley, smiled at her. "It was very impressive to watch you fight so hard to get him out. I mean, don't get me wrong, I was actually hoping the roof would cave in on you both. Save me a ton of trouble. But I have to give you credit for not giving up. You fought like hell, and you managed to get him out." He lifted his hand, and she saw the gleam of a knife's sharp blade. "Your death in the garage would have been easy enough to explain. Not like they've got top notch arson investigators up here. An accident on a cold night. Sad, but shit happens." He sighed, a long and dramatic sound. "Now, though, things are going to have to be different."

John wasn't moving. Wasn't breathing. She was on her knees beside him, and the snow had soaked her jeans. She rose, legs shaking, as she stared at the man she'd trusted for so long. A man who shouldn't be there. "Y-you were in Atlanta."

The fire raged behind him.

"No, I've been here, the whole time." His smile vanished, and his handsome face twisted with rage. "Trying to finish you off, but the fucking hero kept getting in my way."

Devin was the one who'd attacked them? *Devin?*

"The hero's dead now." He took a menacing step toward her. "So that means killing you should be a breeze. So why don't you just be a good girl and come a little bit closer…"

"Fuck you," Shelly cried, the words a rough rasp as they broke from her. Then she ran, she rushed away from him and headed toward the driveway. She just had to get to the road. Had to find the deputy who was watching her place. If she could get to him…

"Shelly!" Devin screamed after her. "There's nowhere to run. No one to help you!"

She didn't stop. She just ran faster.

And Devin's laughter followed behind her.

***

Shelly was absolutely fucking adorable. She was running away, leaving giant tracks in the snow for him to follow. Acting as if she still had a chance.

She didn't.

Shelly thought a deputy was waiting down the road. He knew what she intended to do. Get to the deputy. Get help.

But the deputy was long gone. He'd already taken care of the fellow.

He'd eliminated all of the obstacles in his way.

Devin glared down at John Smith's body. He'd killed that bastard once before. Or at least, he thought he had. "This time," Devin muttered, "let's just make absolutely sure." And he drove his knife into John's heart. Shoved it down with all of his strength.

John still didn't move.

Devin stared at John's face. "Told Charles you were too close to Shelly. It's those fucking eyes of hers. Dark and deep. Sexy as shit." He yanked the knife back. Saw blood drip from the edge. "At least you got to fuck her this time." He stood to his full height. "Don't worry, I'll try to make it quick for her. I always had a bit of a soft spot for Charles's little sister." Smiling, he turned and began to run after Shelly.

He did enjoy a good hunt.

CHAPTER TEN

Her feet sank into the snow, but Shelly trudged on as fast as she could. She knew where the deputy's car was stationed — Blane had told her exactly where the guy would be. She just didn't understand why the deputy hadn't already come rushing to help her. He must have seen the flames.

She'd run to get help from him — and she'd also run so that Devin would follow her. If he followed her, then he'd leave John alone. John could do — well, whatever the hell it was that he did when he came back from the dead. *And you have to come back, John.* She wouldn't let herself think of anything else. He *would* come back. She couldn't lose him.

She rounded the curve, lungs aching, a stitch cutting into her side, breath heaving, and she glimpsed the back of the deputy's vehicle. The moon hung in the sky, surrounded by glittering stars, providing enough light for her to see the cruiser. The vehicle's bumper was positioned just behind the row of trees. Shelly risked a fast glance over her shoulder.

Devin. He's coming.

She pushed herself faster, lunging through the snow. Her hands slapped against the side of the driver's door. Through the slightly foggy window, she could see the deputy sitting inside. "Help me!" Why wasn't he getting out of the car? "Help—" She yanked at the handle.

The door opened. The vehicle's interior light immediately brightened the car. She saw exactly why the deputy hadn't helped her.

Blood soaked his chest. His eyes were closed. Her hands flew over him, going to his neck, and she felt the faintest beat of his pulse beneath her touch. Still alive. For the moment. She dove across him, grabbing for the radio in the car. "Help, help!" Her voice was too rough and weak. She cleared her throat, tried again. "This is Shelly Hampton and—"

Nothing was happening. She tugged on the radio's wire and realized it had been sliced apart. Furious, she threw the radio against the dash. Her hands slid over the deputy's body. "I'm so sorry," she whispered to him. "I need your gun. I'll get the gun and then I'll help us both—"

"Looking for his gun?" Devin called out. "Don't waste your time. I've got it."

He was still a few feet away. She looked back at him. Then she jumped fully into the car, yanking the door shut behind her. She locked the doors with one fast press of a button, and Shelly had to crawl over the deputy's slumped form, apologizing all the while. But at least she'd just bought a little time. Now she could find the keys. She could drive—

A gunshot fired into the passenger side window. Glass exploded, and Shelly screamed.

Then Devin's hand was shoving through the broken glass. He unlocked the door, and she kicked him, pounding at him so that he'd get back. But he just caught her kicking legs and dragged her out of the car. Her head hit the ground and for a moment, Shelly saw stars.

When the stars faded, Devin loomed over her.

"Why?" Shelly demanded. Why was he doing this? She'd trusted him. Her brother had *trusted* him.

"The oldest reason in the world, Shelly sweetheart. Money. Guess who will get everything now that you're gone?"

She wasn't gone, not yet. "S-someone will...figure it out." He'd left a trail of destruction at her cabin. There was no way that people would just think—

He bent down in front of her. He'd tucked the gun into his jeans, and he once again held the knife in his hands. "No one will figure anything out. You see, I didn't do any of this tonight. *I'm* still in Atlanta. Got a dozen witnesses ready to swear to that fact. Of course, I *paid* those people, but what the hell ever, right?" He slid the knife's blade beneath her chin. "I didn't do this," he said again. "When Sheriff Blane finally gets here and finds your dead body, when he finds the dead deputy…"

The deputy isn't dead yet. But she clamped her lips together and didn't say a word.

"He'll think your lover did the job. John Smith. After all, the guy always was a freaking psycho."

"S-says the man with the knife at my throat." The cold was making her shiver. The cold and the terror.

Devin laughed and hauled Shelly to her feet. "I served with John, back in the day. Did you know that? I'm the one who recommended him to your brother. Knew I'd be able to keep tabs on him, and I understood how he worked." The knife bit into her throat. "But the guy went fucking wild for you. Couldn't believe that shit. The untouchable iceman had fallen in love with a girl he hadn't even talked to. Fucking hell. Then he had protective instincts times damn one hundred. He started edging too close to the truth. Getting too suspicious. He had to be eliminated."

The truth…"You killed my brother."

"Did I?" Devin laughed. Then he pushed her up against the side of the deputy's car. The knife was right over her jugular. "This is how the scene will play out. You're going to die. But not here, I can't have the blood spilling here because that won't mesh with the story I've got planned. I'm going to take you back to your lover. You'll die right next to him. Because, see, Sheriff Blane will tell the world that John killed you. John's prints will be on the weapon…"

She realized that Devin was wearing gloves. He'd just slid the fingers of his left hand over her cheek, and she'd felt the leather against her skin.

"Don't worry, though," Devin added. "You fight back in this scene. You stab your lover. Unfortunately, in the end, you both die."

"Blane won't believe…"

"He's a small town, hick sheriff. He'll have his bad guy wrapped up in a bow. End of story. End of you, Shelly."

She had to get away from him. "I'm not going to walk with you back to the cabin." Her words ripped out. "You think I'll just follow along meekly to my death?"

"No, I figured I'd just knock your sweet ass out." He pulled back the knife. Shoved it into a sheath on his belt. His hand fisted and —

She kneed him in the groin. As hard as she could. Devin bellowed, his hand flying out, but she ducked and raced by him. The trees were up ahead. Maybe she could get a branch and use it as a weapon. Maybe she could —

He tackled her. They both hit the snow and she sank into it, sliding down into the cold. He crushed her, using the weight of his body to hold her down. Devin, the man who'd been her brother's best friend. The man who'd gone to countless dinners with her. The man who'd taken her and her brother out to ball games, to concerts, to—

He flipped her over in the snow. One of his hands was at her throat. The other had drawn back into a fist. "It's better this way," he told her, and his voice was gruff. "After this hit, you won't feel a thing."

She clawed at the hand around her neck.

"And I won't have to look into your eyes when I kill you."

She tried to speak, tried to gasp out his name, but couldn't.

His fist flew toward her, but...but it didn't make contact.

Because Devin's fist had been caught, barely an inch from her face. Eyes wide and terrified, she stared up—at John.

"No one kills her." John's fingers surrounded Devin's. He squeezed, and Shelly heard the snap of bones. She knew John had just crushed Devin's hand as the other man screamed in agony.

Then John was jerking Devin off her. Wrenching the guy to his feet and Shelly was sucking in a desperate gulp of air. Her throat burned, and she put her hand to it—a hand wet from the snow.

Devin took a swing at John, but John easily dodged the move. Then his fist slammed into Devin's nose. *Crack.* Blood spurted down Devin's face.

"You sonofabitch," Devin snarled. He yanked out his knife. Held it tightly in his hand. "What the fuck happened? Did I miss your heart? How many freaking lives do you have left?"

John had circled so that he stood in front of Shelly. "More than you do," he snapped back. "You're dying. You were a dead man the minute you went after her."

"Playing the noble card? That shit doesn't work with me. I *know* you, John. You wanted to fuck her from the first moment you saw her. Your MO…use 'em, and walk away. So why don't you do us both a favor…*walk*. Right now. Forget this night. I'll make it worth your while, man." Devin's words came out fast as he shifted from foot to foot. "Look, just calm down a minute. It's me. Your old buddy, Devin. We've been through some rough shit together—"

"You tried to kill me." John's voice was a lethal growl.

"That was a mistake." Devin gave a nervous laugh. "I'm not looking to kill you now. I'm looking to offer you a deal. Five hundred thousand dollars. To just turn your back and forget this night. To forget her."

Shelly was on her feet and looking for a weapon. She spied a heavy branch a few feet away, and she scrambled for it.

"I'm sorry about what happened before, but you were in my way." Devin's words were still coming too fast. "The bodyguard gig is long over, you should have stepped down. But, shit, you just got too hooked on her, didn't you? Look, I know you fucked her already. You did the deed, now *walk*. I'll give you so much money that—"

John didn't give him a chance to finish. He lunged for the other man. Their bodies collided with a heavy thud, and then they were crashing into the snow.

Shelly grabbed the branch and ran toward them. "John!"

But John was already rising to his feet. Brushing the snow off his body. And staring down at Devin. Devin...who had a knife sticking out of his heart.

"See how you like it when someone carves into your chest." John's shoulders heaved. "Only your ass won't be coming back."

Shelly stared at Devin. His fingers were pulling at the handle of the knife—the same knife he'd planned to use on her. But he couldn't get the blade out and his body shuddered. His eyes—rolling, wild—found hers. "Sh-Shelly..."

She still held the branch, gripping it as if her makeshift weapon were a baseball bat.

But Devin didn't get to say anything else. His breath rushed out, and his body stopped shuddering. Devin stilled.

She didn't move. She gripped that branch, and her fingers were absolutely numb as she held it close.

"Baby?"

Her head whipped up. John was gazing at her. John...alive. Strong.

"Are you okay?" John asked carefully.

She dropped the branch. She threw her body against his, and she held him as tightly as she could. "I was afraid you weren't going to come back!" And she'd been freaking terrified. "I got you out of the fire, but then you weren't moving. You weren't breathing. Devin was there, and I wanted him away from you. I wanted you to come back and I—"

He kissed her. Crushed his mouth to hers and pulled her even closer to his body. There was desperation in his kiss. From him. From her. Adrenaline and fear crashed through her body, and she just held on to him. In her mind, she kept thinking...*Alive, he's alive. John's alive. Everything is going to be okay. Everything—*

"I'm alive," he gritted out against her mouth. "Death won't keep me from you." Then his arms were rubbing against hers. "Shit, baby, you're freezing. Let's get you back to the cabin. Get you safe and we'll call the sheriff—"

She shoved against his arms, her eyes widening in horror. "The deputy!" Then she tried to rush around John, but he caught her in his arms, holding her against his body. "John, the deputy in the car—Devin stabbed him, but he's still alive. He needs help!"

John let her go. They hurried back to the car. The deputy had slumped deeper into the seat. The whole car smelled of blood. John put his hands over the man's wounds, trying to stop the flow of blood. Light flooded out from the interior of the car.

"The radio doesn't work," Shelly said as shivers slid over her body. She couldn't seem to stop shaking. "I-I need to go back to the cabin and get my phone." She vaguely remembered putting it down before she'd gone upstairs. "I can call for help. I can—"

But John's head whipped to the side. He stared out at the darkness. "I hear a siren. Still some distance away."

Had to be, because she didn't hear a damn thing.

"But help is coming, baby. It's on the way." He nodded to her. "You flag them down. I'll stay with the deputy."

Her gaze slid toward the darkness. Fear snaked through her.

"You're safe," John assured her. "Devin is dead."

"He was my friend." Her body was still trembling. From the cold? From fear? From the horror of what had just happened? She didn't know. "He was my brother's friend. But I think he killed Charles."

"He won't hurt you ever again. He isn't going to hurt anyone else." John was still pushing against the wounds on the deputy's chest. "He's gone, Shelly. You're safe now."

Her breath came too fast. "He said he knew you. Did you recognize him?"

John just shook his head.

And she could finally hear the faint wail of the sirens. Still in the distance. She stayed with John, trying to help the deputy, until the sirens grew louder. Closer. And when they did, when the lights swept toward them, she rushed to wave down the cars.

Soon the area was swarming with the local authorities. Blane ran to her, pulling her into his arms. "Shelly, shit, I got reports from folks halfway down the mountain. They saw the fire—"

"I'm okay." She wasn't, though. But a good lie was needed right then. He didn't need to know how close to breaking she was. "We…John stopped…he stopped the man who was trying to kill me."

John was beside her. EMTs were working on the injured deputy.

Blane let Shelly go, and he stepped back, his gaze sweeping over John. "That's a whole lot of blood."

John didn't speak.

"Where is the attacker?" Blane demanded. "Where—"

"It was Devin," Shelly cut in. "Devin Donley."

"Your brother's partner?" Blane's voice was heavy with shock.

Blane knew Devin. Devin had been to the cabin before. He'd come with them on summer vacations. He'd been a *friend*.

He'd also been a killer. But now… "He's dead," Shelly said. And she wanted to be very, very clear on this part. "John killed Devin in order to save my life."

Blane swore, then he hurried past her.

She stood there, trapped in the swirl of lights, her body absolutely ice cold. She didn't know how long she'd been out in the cold. Her teeth were chattering. Maybe she should go find a coat. Shelly took a step forward and almost fell face-first into the snow.

But John caught her. He pulled her into his arms, lifting her easily. Her face slid into the crook of his neck. He was so warm.

"I've got you," John whispered.

She remembered what it had been like when he was so still on the ground. When she'd touched him and found no heartbeat.

Her tears came and she couldn't stop them.

"I've got you," he told her once more as he held her tighter.

CHAPTER ELEVEN

He'd almost lost her.

John walked out of the small bathroom, tendrils of steam following him. Long hours had passed since the hell on that mountain. He'd answered dozens of questions for the sheriff. He'd gone over the attack again and again during a night that never seemed to end.

The nightmare was over now. Shelly's attacker — *his* attacker — was out of the picture. They were both safe.

He hadn't wanted to stay at the cabin that night. After everything that had happened, John had thought Shelly needed to escape for a little while, too. And since the place had been swarming with deputies and fire fighters, getting out had seemed like the best plan.

For the time being, they were in the apartment over Sammy's bar. The same damn bar he'd been thrown out of his first day in town. Sammy had offered the place to Shelly, and she'd accepted. She'd been so quiet. So withdrawn, and the pain on her face absolutely ripped John apart.

He strode into the bedroom. Sparsely furnished, but with a big, wooden bed that dominated the space. A patchwork quilt covered the bed, and Shelly sat on it, her shoulders hunched, her head down. Like him, she'd taken a shower, and her long hair — still wet — hung over her shoulders. A fire crackled in the nearby fireplace.

John stilled when he saw her. And he remembered the absolute terror he'd felt when he'd woken on the cold ground, and she'd been gone. An ache had burned in his chest, right over his heart. Ice had encased his body, but the burning in his chest had kept getting stronger and stronger until he'd broken through that ice. He'd jumped up and seen the wreckage of the garage. Seen those flames shooting so high into the sky. He didn't remember getting out of the blaze. Now, he knew exactly *why* he didn't remember. "You pulled me out of the fire."

She flinched at his voice. Dawn was coming. Dawn, finally. He could see the streaks of light trying to push through the blinds.

He stepped toward her. The wooden floor was covered with a thick, dark rug. "You went into the garage, when it was burning, and you got me out."

Her head lifted. Her dark gaze met his. There was pain in her stare. Grief. "I didn't know if you could come back, not if your body was burned.

And I couldn't leave you. I had to save you." Her lower lip trembled. "But when I got you out, you were so still. Your heart wasn't beating, and then Devin was just there."

"He fucking stabbed me in the heart." His hand rose to his chest. The skin was still red.

Shelly jumped to her feet. She wore a heavy, blue robe. One that Sammy had given to her. She came toward him and the robe swirled around her feet. She put her hand to his chest.

He was clad only in a towel, one he'd knotted around his waist. So her fingers brushed against his bare skin, seeming to sear him straight to his soul.

"I thought he'd run after me," she said, voice husky. "That it would give you a chance to heal."

"Guess he wanted to make sure I was dead first."

Her gaze met his. Her touch lingered on his chest. "I think he killed my brother."

Yeah, it sure as hell looked that way.

"And I think…back in Miami…I think he may have killed you, too."

Rage twisted inside of John.

"Devin said that he served with you. We can pull your military records, John. We can find out more about your life. We can retrace your footsteps, can see who you were."

He stepped away from her. "On the phone…back at the cabin, Devin said I was obsessed with you."

Her lips twisted. "I think it's safe to say that the man was a liar *and* a killer."

"When I escaped the lab, I came straight to you. You've been in my head for months—"

Once more, she closed the distance between them. "Because you knew—deep inside—you knew I was in danger. You found me because you were coming to help me. And you did. You saved me. You saved that deputy. My brother's killer isn't going to be on the streets any longer. All because of you."

"I killed a man." And he'd done it so easily. Hadn't hesitated. Because when Devin had targeted Shelly…*I knew I wasn't going to let him live.*

"Am I supposed to be afraid of you because of that? I'm not. I've never been more grateful than when I saw you standing over me."

But she was still painting him as a hero, and he wasn't sure that he was. "It was too easy to kill." And something that he knew—*I think I've done it before.*

"Devin didn't give you a choice. If you hadn't stopped him, he was going to kill me. He was going to stab me and leave my body at the cabin."

Rage flared hotter and harder inside of him. *Not her. Never her.*

"Devin was right in front of me, all these years, and I didn't see the monster staring back at me."

John was the one staring at her right then. What did she see, when she looked at him?

The fire crackled, and he jerked. His gaze slid to the flames in the fireplace. His fingers flexed, stretching, then fisting. "You shouldn't have come into that garage." He now knew that Devin had rigged the place to blow. Tricky bastard. Devin had stayed back, safe from a distance, and he'd detonated when John went inside. "You could have been killed in there."

"Maybe I wanted a turn at trying to save you."

His gaze flew back to her. A faint smile curved her lips, but as he gazed down at her, the smile slipped away. She shook her head. "No, no, that's not what happened." Her chin lifted. "I heard the explosion. When I got outside, I saw the flames. I knew you were inside, and nothing on this earth would have made me leave you there. I get that you're super strong and pretty much indestructible, but you were *burning*. I couldn't leave you to burn. I couldn't do that."

"Shelly…"

"Maybe I'm the one who's obsessed," she murmured. "I'm the one in too deep. Because I swear, John, I've never felt this way about anyone before. I felt like my heart was being ripped out of my chest when I saw those flames. I got inside, and there was so much smoke. The fire was everywhere. There were boards on your legs, and they were on fire, and I couldn't get you to wake up."

He caught her hands in his. Saw the bruises and the scratches and the blisters on her fingers. He'd healed, but she hadn't. She carried the pain on her. He brought her hands to his mouth. Pressed tender kisses to her skin. "Thank you."

"John?"

He lifted her into his arms. Took her to the bed. "When I was in that fucking lab, I used to think...someone is going to come. I'm not going to be locked in this hell-hole forever. Someone will remember me. Someone will get me out of here." He eased her onto the bed. Sat down next to her. Caged her with his arms. "You're that someone, Shelly."

"I didn't." A furrow was between her brows. "I didn't know—"

"You walked through fire for me tonight, baby. If you'd known I was in that lab, you would have torn the place apart in order to get to me."

She nodded. "Yes." And the truth was there, right between them. Emotions that neither of them quite understood, but a connection that bound them nonetheless.

He'd fight for her. Kill for her. He *had* killed for her.

And she'd gone into the fire for him.

His gaze searched hers. "I'm sorry about your brother."

Her lips trembled. "I was preparing to bury him while you were dying."

"I'm not dead." He had another chance. A chance with her. A chance at a life, and he was going to grab it tight with both hands.

But it was her soft hand that rose. Her hand that curled under his jaw. "You're not dead." Her hand trailed down his chest. Stilled over his heart. "I can feel it beating again."

His heart was beating even faster, for her.

"Where do you go, when your heart stops?"

He wasn't sure. Sometimes, he had brief flashes. Images. Bursts of light. Sometimes, John swore that he saw her.

"I want you to try reading my mind again," Shelly told him.

John hesitated. "I thought you told me to stay out of your head."

"I want you to know what I'm feeling, what I'm wanting, right now."

But he didn't ease the safeguards he'd put in his mind. Instead, his head bent toward her. His mouth hovered over hers. "Tell me what you want, and it's yours."

"You. I just want you."

He knew she was coming off an emotional landslide. Devin, the attack, her brother…John didn't want to slip into her mind because later, she'd hate the invasion. When her pain eased and when the adrenaline left her, she'd be angry that he'd seen her most private thoughts.

"Do you want me, John?"

His cock was full and heavy, shoving against the towel that tried to confine him. "Baby, I always want you." She didn't need to be a mind reader in order to know that. "But you've been through hell today, you don't need—"

"You *are* what I need. You're what I want." Her fingertips skimmed down his stomach. Down to the towel. "Will you make love to me?"

He kissed her. Took her mouth. Let go of the iron control he'd held so tightly in the hours after the chaos on that mountain. Her lips parted for him. Her tongue met his. The kiss was harder than it should have been. He needed to exercise care with her, but a dark demon had been riding within him.

What if he hadn't woken up soon enough?

What if he hadn't healed soon enough?

What if he hadn't gotten to her in those damn woods soon enough?

When he'd arrived, Devin had been about to drive his fist into her delicate jaw. What would have come next?

The bastard's knife in her throat?

Can't lose her. Won't. Shelly was the reason he'd kept going. The reason he'd survived the lab.

His kiss was desperate. His hands were shaking as they held her. He could barely keep himself in check, and John knew he should be exercising more caution. Giving her pleasure. Stroking her. Caressing her. But at the touch of her mouth against his, everything changed.

He rolled on the bed, bringing her on top of him, knowing that the position would give her more power. Her knees were on either side of his hips. The robe had parted, and her sex pushed against his cock. Her naked sex. She wasn't wearing panties. Sweet fuck.

He yanked at the belt of the robe and the robe parted, revealing her tight nipples, those perfect breasts. He leaned up and took one into his mouth even as his hand slid between their bodies.

Get her ready. Don't take. Get —

His fingers slid over her sex. Pushed against her clit. Had her moaning against him. Arching.

"I don't want to wait," Shelly gasped. "Don't make me wait."

He was already at the edge. And her voice, her sexy plea…no, he'd never make her wait. He positioned his cock and drove deep into her with one hard thrust. Her head tipped back, her eyes closed.

He nearly lost his mind. She was so tight and hot. Perfect paradise.

Then Shelly lifted her body up, only to push back down.

His hands flew up and grabbed the headboard. He heard the creak of the wood. He held the wood tight while she rode him, her cheeks flushed, her lips parted, her body so eager and sexy.

He tried to hold back. Tried to let her take the lead but…

"John!"

He rolled them again, and this time, he was on top. She came beneath him, her body bucking as the pleasure poured through her, and he let go. His climax slammed through his body, and his breath heaved out. He pressed his mouth to her neck. Kissing her, marking her, fucking loving her as he came. The orgasm went on and on, and when it was done, when he was finished…

He lifted his head. Stared down at Shelly. And realized—"Fuck, baby, I didn't use anything."

Her smile came, went, but left a faint glow in her eyes. "It's okay, I'm covered. And I wanted to be this way with you."

"Shelly...I..." He was already getting hard inside of her again. Because he craved her, endlessly.

"I'm clean," she said, and her words hitched a bit as she pushed her hips up against him. "And I'm figuring if you can heal from any injury, well, you're probably clean, too."

He pushed into her, loving the way her body tightened around him. Slick and hot. Heaven.

"Again?" Shelly asked, her voice the purest temptation he'd ever heard.

Again. Always. He withdrew, pushed back, and when she moaned for him, he felt like Christmas had just fucking come. His dream was in his arms. She was holding him, arching up to him, giving him her sweet body, and she stared at him with shining eyes, wanting him, needing him, just as wildly as he needed her.

John kissed her and he fucked her, and he knew he'd always want her. He wanted her pleasure, her whispers, her dreams. He wanted every single thing about her.

His mouth trailed over her neck. Over her silken skin. She gasped and quivered. Oh, hell, yes, she liked that spot. He made a mental note to always kiss her right there, on the curve of her shoulder. Then he slid down, his fingers teasing her breasts. Her legs locked around his hips as she gave a quick cry of his name.

His name on her lips. A *name*. Not a number. He was John. And Shelly—Shelly was his. A woman who wanted him. Needed him.

Loved him?

Hell, no, probably not yet, but maybe...maybe one day.

She came again, crying out his name once more, and he followed her, driving into her, over and over again, until the climax ripped through him. Until she was all he knew.

All he wanted.

***

"She's going to die..."

He couldn't move. John was on the ground, twisted on his side. Dirt and grime were all around him, and his chest felt ice cold. Car horns sounded in the distance, and he could see the faint green edge of a dumpster.

"You thought you'd play the hero, didn't you?" That taunting voice demanded. Shoes were in front of his face. Black boots. "But you're just going to die." The guy crouched in front of him. He recognized the bastard's face.

Devin. Devin Donley.

"You always thought you were better than me, didn't you? The better soldier. The better fighter. The better fucking man." Devin stared at the bloody knife in his hand. "Guess who's better now, old friend? And when I have all of her money, when that company is mine, no one will ever fucking think I wasn't good enough."

Devin was going to kill Shelly. "Sh…Sh…" John couldn't talk.

"There's a whole lot of blood pumping out of you. Guess you didn't think this was how it would end, did you? That's why it was so easy. You always looked for a threat from the outside. You thought you were protecting her from someone else." Devin smiled. "That's the thing with people. They never see the real danger, not when it's up close. That's why Shelly hasn't known. Why she'll have no clue when I come for her. Maybe I'll use the same knife on her. Think that's fitting, don't you?" Devin rose.

John's fingers slid toward him, creeping along the grime and dirt and blood.

"It's taking you a fucking long time to die." Devin drove his boot into John's side. "Maybe let's just speed this shit up."

The knife came at him again. Sinking into him, driving deep. Fast. Hard.

"You loved her, didn't you, John? The mighty John finally fell. Too bad, she'll never know."

A siren screamed in the night.

"Fuck," Devin muttered. Then he was running away. His feet thudded across the broken pavement.

John tried to move. Tried to drag himself forward, but his whole body was numb. A pool of blood surrounded him. He knew he was dying. He could feel it. And if he died...

What about Shelly?

Shelly...

He had to help her. Had to —

***

John jerked upright. His heart was pounding and sweat covered his body. Immediately, he reached to the side, needing to touch Shelly, needing to make sure that she was still close. But she wasn't there.

His head turned. Shelly stood at the window, gazing out at the street. Sunlight spilled in, creating a soft glow around her.

John sucked in a deep breath. One, then another. He knew he'd just had another memory. This time, it had been a memory of his death. When he was close to Shelly, fuck, the memories came more often. They were stronger.

"It's not fair."

Her voice was low, soft.

He slid from the bed. Grabbed a pair of jeans and jerked them on. "Baby?"

She turned toward him. "I'm sorry."

He shook his head, having no idea what she was talking about.

"I haven't been fair to you." She closed the distance between them. "You came into my life, and you just wanted to help me. I was afraid of you at first. I doubted you, and because of me, you were nearly blown up." Her hand pressed over his heart. "You were stabbed."

"You know it takes a lot to stop me." Because of whatever had been done to him. A science experiment gone so wrong.

Her gaze searched his. "I was looking out the window. And I saw people — families, couples — they're walking down the street. Laughing. Shopping. Christmas is just a few days away."

His brow furrowed. Where was she going with this?

"I woke up, I woke up safe and alive and in your arms — and I realized I haven't been fair to you."

"Shelly —"

"I wasn't celebrating Christmas because it hurt me to remember the past. It hurt to remember what I lost. But you've lost more than I have. And you still keep going. You keep fighting. You don't give up."

He would never give up on her.

"And I won't give up, either," she promised. She gave him a quick smile. "Things haven't been fair to you, but I'm going to change that. I just, I swear, I almost feel like Scrooge. In the story, when he looks out the window and realizes that he didn't miss Christmas? That's me, right now. I looked out the window, I looked out the window and realized there was still time." Her words were coming faster now. "Because of you, I still have time. *We* have time. The past is gone, but we can start new. We can make new memories. We can make better memories, and we can do it together."

"You're not Scrooge," John told her, even as he felt his own lips kick into a slow smile.

Her gaze held his. "But you are my Christmas."

That was…shit, now his chest was aching, right beneath her touch.

"I didn't miss you. I didn't miss the chance to know you. I won't miss anything with you again. And I'm not going to drag you down into pain and sadness with me. It's not fair," she said again. "Instead, we're going to celebrate. We are going to be happy. Just like all of those people out on the street. We are going to be—"

His arms wrapped around her. John pulled Shelly up against him. He lifted her and held her easily as his mouth took hers. Not in a fierce, demanding kiss, but soft. Caressing. Tender. With her, he could be tender.

"Happy," she whispered against his mouth. "We're going to be happy."

He was happy right the hell then. What he'd been through, the damn lab, the battles, they didn't matter. He had her. "You don't need to pretend for me." He knew how much she hurt. "I don't need whatever you think those people outside have. I don't need —"

"You need to make good memories. And memories are what I want to give to you."

He slowly lowered her until her feet touched the floor. "Baby…"

Her smile lit her face. Made her eyes shine. Made him want to give her the absolute world. "Will you have Christmas with me, John?" Shelly asked him, the words coming in a fast, eager rush.

Hell, yes. Didn't the woman get it? He'd do anything, give her anything. He cleared his throat and said, "I think that maybe we should start with a tree."

And if anything, her smile became even bigger.

Right then, everything made sense to him. And he realized that Devin — dead bastard that he was — the guy had been right about one thing.

John did love Shelly. He didn't know when it had happened, but he knew why she'd been the one person he remembered. Why she was able to crack through the darkness in his mind and give him slivers of his past.

Because what he felt for her went beyond the moment. It went beyond just a memory. She'd worked her way into his heart. His soul.

And she was always going to stay there.

CHAPTER TWELVE

"Is the tree okay?" Shelly asked as she tilted her head and studied the slightly…well, sickly tree that was left in the lot. Christmas was right around the corner, so she shouldn't have been surprised by the slim pickings left in town.

But she didn't want John to be disappointed. She was absolutely determined to give him the best possible holiday. After all, what else could she give him? He'd done so much for her, she owed him something magical in return.

Only the tree didn't exactly look magical.

Shelly glanced over her shoulder. John was standing next to the red and white entrance post for the tree lot. A post that had been painted to resemble a candy cane. Christmas lights covered the top of the post, blinking in a slow rhythm.

"Perfect," John told her quietly. Only, he wasn't look at the tree. He was looking at her.

Shelly felt her cheeks burn. "It's really not." And the tree was definitely not what she'd had in mind for their first Christmas together. For the first Christmas that John would ever remember.

Things had already been bad enough with the attacks and the fire and Devin's death. She just wanted to turn things around so badly.

"Ah, Ms. Shelly?" The owner of the tree lot sidled closer to her as he sensed a sale. "Want me to have that delivered up to your cabin?"

The owner was a real sweetheart of a man named Jebidiah Crow. He knew what had happened at her place—all of the locals did, and everyone was treating her with extra kindness. They made her feel safe. They made her feel loved.

They made her feel like things were going to get better.

"We absolutely want that tree," John said before Shelly could reply. He stalked forward. His hand caught hers, and he threaded his fingers with hers. She was wearing gloves, hoping to protect the blisters and cuts on her fingers. His hands were bare. But she could feel the warmth of his touch through her glove. "And we'd very much appreciate it if you took it to the cabin for us."

Because they'd been given the all-clear by Blane. They could go back to the cabin. The remains of the garage were roped off, Blane had told them that he had yellow tape all around the place. But they could enter the cabin once more.

No more sleeping over Sammy's bar.

"Let's go for a walk," John murmured. His gaze was so watchful on her.

She gave him a quick smile and tried to forget about the tree and its bald spots. She had plenty of ornaments at the cabin. She could hide those spots. She could make things work.

She *would* make it work.

A school chorus group was stationed on the corner, all the kids dressed in matching red tops and wearing Santa hats. They were singing as she and John passed them, and the sound was so sweet and happy. The kids didn't look afraid. They didn't look worried.

That was what she wanted. She wanted that kind of joy for John.

"We don't have to do this," John said. He'd slid ever closer to her. "You don't need to pretend with me."

Her head turned. "Pretend?" Her voice was a bare whisper because she didn't want to interrupt the singers.

"Things have been hard. I know you're hurting. You don't have to act like you're—"

"I want this holiday with you." Devin had destroyed enough. Taken enough from her. She was determined to take her life back.

His head inclined toward her. "Then we'll have the holiday. We'll have anything you want."

Almost anything because she still had the small problem of needing to get him a present. Something that he'd enjoy.

They started walking again. He was holding her hand, and snow was on the ground all around them. People were laughing. It seemed so incredibly normal, and she wanted to be a part of that *normal* world.

Sammy's bar waited up ahead.

"Let's get our bags," Shelly decided as they kept walking. "And then we can go home. We can get there before Jeb, and then put up the tree."

He turned her in his arms. Stood right there, in front of the entrance to Sammy's. "Home," John repeated that one word, and his whole face tensed.

Had she said the wrong thing? "I didn't mean…" Her words trailed away. What had she meant?

"I think you are my home, Shelly."

That was…his words were making her heart melt.

Before she could respond, the door opened with a jingle and Sammy stood there. He saw them, and he immediately put his hands on his hips. "You know the rules," Sammy barked.

Rules? What—

Then Sammy's index finger pointed up. "If you're under the mistletoe, you have to kiss."

Shelly glanced up. Sure enough, a sprig of mistletoe hung right above her.

"I'm all for obeying the rules." John pulled her closer. His hand slid under her chin as he tipped back her head. "Merry Christmas, sweetheart."

He kissed her. Such a sweet, tender kiss. Light and gentle. As if she were the most delicate thing in the world. As if...

As if she were the most *important* thing in his world.

His head lifted. He gazed into her eyes. She held her breath, wondering what he'd say...

John smiled at her. "We need to take some of that mistletoe home with us." There had been just the faintest emphasis on *home*.

Sammy laughed. "You're smarter than I thought, boy."

John wasn't exactly a boy.

She glanced at Sammy. He inclined his head toward her and John. "I was wrong about you." The humor had slipped from Sammy's face as his gaze sharpened on John. "Thought you were trouble when I first saw you. Didn't want you around Shelly." He offered his hand to John. "Thank you for looking out for her."

John took his hand. Shook it. "Thank *you* for looking out for her. She's damn special, and I'm glad she has people like you in her life."

They headed back into the bar. John went upstairs to grab their bags, and she stayed below, lingering with Sammy as he served up drinks. Evening was sliding up on them, and that meant more customers for Sammy.

Holiday music blasted from the speakers, and Sammy was putting whipped cream on the top of all the drinks he made, calling them "snow-capped" as the patrons laughed.

Her fingers tapped on the bar top, moving in beat with the music. The tension slid from her body. Sammy winked at her as he slid a snow-capped drink her way. "You remind me of your father so much."

The ache came and went in her heart.

"Like you, he'd have his serious moments. He'd work, get so fixated with Blane's dad as they tried to come up with their inventions." He laughed. "Thought the guy would never do anything but work, and then he met your mom. Met her right here in this bar." His hands swept out. "And I knew then, his life wasn't going to be the same." He reached across the bar and squeezed her hand. His gaze had turned knowing. "Your life isn't going to be the same, either, is it?"

No, not since she'd found John.

"I'll still be stopping by on Christmas Day," Sammy told her with a firm nod. "Make sure there's room at the table."

Someone called his name, and Sammy turned away. She slid onto a barstool, her gaze darting toward the staircase that led to the little apartment upstairs. It would be nice to slip away from the crowd. To get back to the cabin where it would just be her and John. The burned wreckage of the garage wasn't quite gonna thrill her but...

"Excuse me." A male voice rumbled beside her. "I think we need to talk."

Her stare jerked toward the speaker. She found herself staring at a tall, blond-haired man. His hair was a little long, his gaze intense, and a heavy, black coat covered him.

"I'm with someone," Shelly said simply. "But I hope you have a good—"

"You're Shelly Hampton."

Okay, now alarm skittered down her spine.

"My name is Jay Maverick."

The name rang a distant bell. Maverick...Maverick... "The tech guy?"

Jay Maverick was *the* tech darling at the moment. She tilted her head, studying him, yes, she did think she'd seen his face on the cover of a few magazines lately. Why was he in Sammy's?

"It's about John Smith." Jay glanced over his shoulder. Nervous energy clung to him. "We *really* need to talk, but can we do it someplace where there aren't so many people around?"

The faint alarm she'd felt got one hundred times worse. "How do you know John?"

"Your story — what happened with you here, the attacks, I read about it all online. I need to see John. Where is he?"

Her lips clamped together. She didn't know this guy, other than seeing his face on some flashy magazines. And he might be a genius, but he also had a reputation for being wild. For being a playboy. For being trouble.

"This guy bothering you?" Sammy's gravelly voice demanded.

Jay Maverick was asking about John. He was making her nervous. So... "Yes." Shelly gave a hard nod of her head. "I think he needs to leave."

Jay's mouth dropped open. "Wait? What? No, I—"

But Sammy had already snapped his fingers, and the local guys nearby were only too happy to show Jay to the door. She didn't wait around to see if he tried to get back inside. She hurried for the stairs, just as John was striding down. She grabbed his hand. "Let's go out the back." She'd tell him about Jay soon enough. Right then, she wanted to get *out* of that place. Their rental vehicle was out back. They'd get in, get away, and then she could figure out what the hell Jay Maverick wanted with John.

A few moments later, they were behind the bar. The wind blew hard against her as John loaded the bags. He slammed shut the back of the SUV and turned toward her. He smiled but…froze. She saw a heavy tension sweep through him. "John?"

He lunged toward her, putting himself in front of her body. He pushed her behind him as he faced off against some unseen foe. "Who the fuck is there?" John snarled, staring into the shadows near the line of trees.

Her fingers pressed to his back. "Someone was in the bar, asking about you," she whispered.

"And some bastard is hiding in the trees, watching us right now." John's voice rose as he shouted, "Don't make me drag your ass out!"

She rather liked the option of just getting in the vehicle and driving away but…

John's head jerked to the right. "And someone else is coming around the building."

She craned her neck to see around John. A few moments later, Jay Maverick hurried around the building. The spotlights from the back of the bar lit up the scene. And they clearly showed Jay's surprise when he drew up short. His hands lifted. "Whoa! Whoa! Why are you in battle-mode, man?"

John's body was rock hard in front of Shelly. His hands were powerful fists at his sides. Definitely battle-mode.

"I'm not your enemy," Jay assured him quickly. He kept his hands up. "I can help you. At least, I hope I can."

"And the asshole in the woods? The guy watching silently? Is he here to help, too?" John's voice was lethal.

Jay glanced toward the woods. Then he gave a little wave. "Come out, Sawyer! If he sees you, if he sees what you can do, it might calm John down. Get him to *talk* to us."

Shelly peered at the trees. Then she saw a man burst from those trees. A man who was moving far too fast. The same way that John could move too fast. The fellow was almost a blur as he barreled right at John.

Only John leapt forward. He drove his fist out in a flying punch, and the man who'd been rushing toward John — the guy fell back into the snow.

"Damn." Jay sounded impressed, not upset. "That was a beautiful hit."

In the next breath, John had bunched his hand in Jay's shirt-front. He lifted the guy up into the air. "Who the hell are you?"

"Jay!" Jay gasped out. "Jay Maverick! And I can help you!"

"By sending your goon at me?"

Shelly noticed that the goon in question had risen to his feet. Only he wasn't lunging to attack again. Instead, he was brushing snow off his body. Taking his time.

"You were right, Jay," the goon called out. He didn't sound particularly pissed. Actually, he didn't sound bothered at all. "He is like me."

John tossed Jay. The guy crashed into the snow. John's hands fisted once more. "I'm nothing like either one of you," John denied hotly. "I'm—"

"Lazarus." The one word was almost like a curse as it came from the man who'd stopped brushing the snow off his body. Shelly's gaze swept over him. Tall, muscled, dangerous. His dark hair was cut in a short style similar to John's, and his hard jaw was locked tight.

"What the fuck," John began, voice colder than the snow, "did you just say?"

"I was part of the program, too. Experimented on without my consent. And I woke up in a world I didn't know." The man made no move to advance on John. "My name is Sawyer Cage, and I don't want to fight with you. Jay showed me your story. He found it online—the reporter was talking about how you'd cheated death so many times up here, and when we did a little digging, when we found out that you supposedly died in Miami, too." He shrugged. "It wasn't too hard to realize you must be one of us."

Jay cleared his throat. "And you were ex-military. Lazarus liked to use test subjects like you."

John's head whipped toward him. "Like...me?" Each word seemed torn from him.

"Yeah." It was Sawyer who responded. "They take men like us, men that they can turn into weapons."

"The deadlier, the better," Jay muttered.

Shelly had heard enough. She surged forward, moving to John's side. Her hand grabbed his, held tight. "How do we know you guys aren't *part* of Lazarus?"

Jay flinched.

John swore. "*He* is," he said. And his left hand rose as he pointed at Jay. "Bastard's heartrate just tripled, and he's about to hyperventilate."

"It's not what you think!" Jay cried out quickly. "Shit, shit, calm down, okay? Everyone, *calm down!*"

Sawyer's head turned, just a bit, until he was looking toward the bar. "It would help — really help a lot — if you'd tell your man in the shadows to stand down." His words were directed at John. "I get that you don't trust us. But we are not here to hurt you. Not you, not your lady. If you can hear Jay's heart beating, then that just confirms what I already know. You're one of us."

"I am *not* part of your group."

Sawyer was staring at the side of the bar, where the shadows were thickest. "He's a normal human, and I don't want to hurt him, but I don't like having a gun aimed at me."

Shelly's head whipped toward the bar and the shadows. Who was there?

John's body stayed tense, but he called out, "Sheriff Blane! Come on out!"

Blane was there?

And sure enough, Blane appeared. He rushed toward them with his weapon drawn.

"Oh, great." Jay raked a hand through his already tousled hair even as he rocked forward onto the balls of his feet. "Now local law enforcement is involved. So much for keeping a low profile, Sawyer. I told you we had to handle this with tact."

Sawyer didn't appear concerned. "Tact isn't my strong suit. And I'm not here to bullshit John Smith. I want to help him, and I want to see if he can help me."

Blane advanced, moving into the glare of the building's lights. His weapon was aimed at Sawyer. "What's going on here?"

"Don't want to cause trouble," Sawyer said slowly. "I'm here to try and give John some answers, if he wants to hear them. But this doesn't concern you, Sheriff. You should go back to the bar. Enjoy the night. Walk away."

"Hell, no." Blane's grip tightened on the gun. "If you're here to give answers, to tell John why he can't die, why the guy is so freaking fast I can barely see him move sometimes, then I want to hear this shit, too."

"Oh, hell." Jay's hand dropped to his side. "The sheriff already knows? Low profile, people. Low profile. When you're dealing with paranormal shit like this, you're supposed to keep a low profile."

Paranormal shit. Shelly blew out a slow breath. It immediately fogged before her.

John pulled her closer, wrapping his body around hers. "Shelly's cold. If we're going to talk, then we're going inside."

Only no one moved. Well, Sawyer's gaze dropped—it rested on her. Turned thoughtful. "She's the key, huh? What pulled you out into the open?" Now he sounded really curious. "Did you remember her? Or did you just feel somehow connected with her? Because the primitive instincts, those stay, no matter what. That awareness remains, it's just sometimes buried deep inside."

John's head turned. He gazed at Shelly, and he looked absolutely lost. Her strong warrior, lost, and the sight hurt her. She found herself stepping forward, putting her body in front of his. Wanting, this time, to protect him. "There's an apartment above the bar that we can use,"

Shelly announced briskly. "We'll go up there and talk, and you *will* give John the answers he needs." She glared at the men before her. "And then you'll get your asses out of his life."

Sawyer gave her a quick smile. "Yes, ma'am."

CHAPTER THIRTEEN

"Project Lazarus is a top-secret government experiment. Dead soldiers are taken into the program, their bodies are put through a special preservation process, and then they are injected with the Lazarus serum." Sawyer Cage stood in front of the fireplace with his arms crossed over his chest. His stare never wavered from John's face. "When the subjects wake up, they're stronger than before, faster. Their reflexes are far better, and most of us seem to have psychic bonuses."

John's gaze cut to Shelly. While he was standing, she'd sat on the narrow couch, with Blane at her side. Shelly bit her lower lip. Her eyes were huge.

"Hold up!" Blane raised his hand. "Let's go back a bit. You said when the soldiers 'woke up.' But you mean when they come back to life, don't you? Jesus, this is crazy shit."

Jay was pacing behind the couch. "You can't talk about this stuff, Sheriff. Once we leave this room, it will be as if this conversation never occurred. There are government operatives out there, people who are *hunting* the Lazarus subjects. Their identities must be kept secret." He paused and shot a hard glance at John. "So it would help if you cut down on the public heroics and tried to make it look like you *weren't* superhuman." He tapped his chin. "And you've got to stop using your real name. I can get you a new ID. Get you a new place to live. I can have you out of the country in the hour—"

"I'm not going anywhere." John put his hand on Shelly's shoulder. "I'm home."

Jay's stare dipped between the two of them. "Right." He drew out the one word, then cleared his throat. "Look, Shelly's a bit harder to handle considering her family business is worth millions."

John felt surprise rush through him. "Millions?"

She shrugged beneath his hold. "And that's why Devin wanted all the money for himself."

Shit. *Shit.* Okay, he'd known she was wealthy, but this was a whole new level. And he was a man who still didn't even remember his past. What did he have to offer her?

"John?" She rose, moving to stand in front of him. "What's wrong?"

He shook his head.

"You're not a broke asshole, so don't worry about that," Jay drawled, as if reading his mind.

"You made plenty of investments before your, ah, untimely death in Miami. The investments have been tied up in limbo since your death, but I pulled some strings. Some slightly shady strings, mind you, but I got the wheels spinning. I'll make sure you get what you have coming to you."

John growled as he turned his attention to Jay. "What is your link here? You're not a soldier."

There was no way that guy was ex-military.

Jay shoved back his shoulders. "I'm atoning for some sins, all right? That good enough for you? Better be, 'cause that's all you're getting from me right now." He glanced at the dark watch on his wrist. "And we need to wrap this up. I want to check in with Willow."

Willow. The name rocked through John and in a flash, he found himself across the room, with his hand on Jay's throat, pinning Jay against the wall. "Where. Is. She?"

But Jay glared back at him—and the bastard had pulled out a gun. One that he had pointed at John's head. "I won't betray her. Not fucking ever again. And if you don't get your hands off me, right now, I'll make sure that you stay *permanently dead.* A bullet to the brain will do that to your kind. You won't threaten Willow. You won't—"

"*Stop it!*" Shelly yelled.

And then she was pulling on John's arm. "Just tell him, John."

John wasn't telling that bastard anything. He *was* going to rip the gun from Jay's hand, though. Then maybe pound the shit out of the guy.

Shelly sighed. "John was held in a lab of some sort. He heard the name Willow mentioned by the doctors there."

Jay lowered his gun. "You were with her?"

John saw the guilt flash on the guy's face. *Don't trust this one. Won't ever trust this one.* Rage surged through his mind. It would be so easy to attack Jay.

I get that the idea is tempting. Another voice slipped into John's mind. A voice that sounded exactly like Sawyer Cage. *But I can't let you kill the guy. He's still useful to us.*

John let go of Jay. He whirled to face Sawyer.

The other man smiled at him. "See?" Now Sawyer was speaking out loud. "Told you that we came with psychic bonuses. It's easy for the Lazarus subjects to communicate telepathically with one another."

"Holy shit," Blane said as he staggered to his feet. "I'm going downstairs. I need some drinks to handle this mess." He jerked his head toward them. "I'm off duty. So don't think I'm…ah, hell, forget it. I just need some drinks."

No one spoke again until Blane was gone. The door slammed shut behind him.

John pulled in a slow breath, then released it.

"What other psychic powers do you have?" Jay wanted to know.

Jay was a pain in his ass.

"He can get into my head," Shelly said, voice quiet. "Read my thoughts. I asked him to stop, though, and he did."

Jay whistled. "Interesting." Jay's head cocked. "Does it work just with her, or with everyone?"

"Haven't tried it on everyone," John growled.

"Then do it. Try it on me."

No, he didn't want to fucking try it. "We're done for now." Because he didn't want to hear more. He'd already heard enough. More than enough. He was a dead man walking, a lab experiment. Just as he'd thought.

He and Shelly headed for the door, but Sawyer stepped into their path. "It's scary, when you wake up and you don't know anything. When you don't know anyone. I get that, I've been there."

No, the guy didn't get it. John pulled Shelly closer. "I knew her. I woke up, and I remembered her."

Sawyer's eyes widened. "Then you are one lucky bastard," he stated flatly. "I loved my Elizabeth, and it took far too long for me to find her again."

"Shelly was in danger." John's temples were pounding. "Being...hunted. I had to...save her."

Shelly rose onto her toes. She pressed a kiss to his cheek, and the rage and fear that had been swamping him seemed to ease. "You did, John. You saved me."

But he shook his head. She didn't get it. "No, baby, you saved me." If he hadn't possessed the memory of her, if she hadn't been there to get him through those darkest times, John wasn't sure what the hell he would have done.

"You seem to be handling things better than others." Jay's voice had turned musing. "That's good to know. Glad we don't have to lock your ass up."

"*Jay*," Sawyer snarled.

But John had already spun back to face him. "What?"

Jay winced. "Yeah, so, little note about that...Sawyer and I are searching for all the Lazarus subjects because you guys are absolute killing machines. The fiercest warriors ever created, but turns out, there are a few *negative* side effects to the grand old experiment."

"Like his memory loss," Shelly noted.

Jay nodded. "Yes, that and, um, the fact that the Lazarus test subjects can get overwhelmed by negative emotions. Rage. Fear. Jealousy. They multiply inside of the subjects, and they can lead, ahem..." Another wince from him. "Let's just say we recently tangled with a test subject who had to be stopped, permanently. Because he was…wrong. Sometimes, that happens. When you play with life and death, sometimes the people who come back are wrong in the head."

John's temples pounded even harder. He opened his mouth to reply—

"You're *not* stopping, John. He's not wrong. He's the best man I've met. So just get that shit straight in your head. You do *not* hurt him." Shelly moved her body, putting herself between him and the others. "Now, we're leaving. John and I are going to celebrate the holidays. And you guys—just give us a number or something and we'll contact you when *we're* ready."

Sawyer inclined his head toward John. *I'll be close. You need me, hell, it's not like you even have to call.*

But John didn't reply to the guy. Jay had hurried forward and given Shelly his business card. She took it and then yanked open the apartment door. They hurried down the stairs.

I just want to help you. Sawyer's voice drifted through John's head once more. *I've been where you are. You could use a friend in this world.*

He had a friend, he had Shelly.

They pushed through the crowded bar. He glimpsed the sheriff leaning in close and talking with Sammy. A glass of whiskey was near Blane's elbow.

But John and Shelly didn't stop to talk with the sheriff. Shelly was hurrying outside, and John made sure he was right behind her. They didn't speak again, not until they were in their SUV and heading away from town. And then...

"There's nothing wrong about you." Anger hummed beneath Shelly's words. "Don't listen to that jerk. He didn't know what he was talking about."

The men *did* know about Lazarus.

And Shelly didn't know how hard it was, sometimes, how much control he had to keep in place. His control had slipped—no, it had absolutely obliterated when Devin attacked her. The rage had taken over.

There had been no stopping him.

"John?" Her hand reached out. Her fingers curled over his on the steering wheel. "There's nothing wrong with you."

Was she trying to convince him?

Or did she fear the truth and she was trying to convince herself?

***

"I think that went well...ish," Jay decided as he stared at the closed apartment door. "I mean, I'm breathing. You're breathing. The guy *seemed* sane enough when he left with his, um, girlfriend."

Sawyer growled.

Jay faced him, hands going to his hips. "Okay, *maybe* I shouldn't have told him the part about some of the subjects being wrong, but it was the truth, and you know it. That's why we're hunting them down, and when I came across the report about the trouble up here, when I started my research on John Smith, I knew he was part of Lazarus."

"He's different."

Jay rolled his eyes. "You're all different. Different strengths, same weakness—a bullet to the brain."

"He *remembered* his girl."

"And you remembered Elizabeth, once you got closer to her. Look, I don't handle the physical and medical side of this—that's *your* girlfriend's job, remember?" Because Elizabeth had been the one to first create the Lazarus serum. It had been her baby. A baby that had grown into a real beast. "But maybe the fact that Shelly Hampton was in trouble had something to do with his reaction. You guys are all primitive instincts, aren't you? The urge to protect a mate, to keep her safe when she's in danger—doesn't get more primitive than that." And the primitive memories *were* the ones that remained for the Lazarus subjects.

Sawyer was still glaring at him. "He might not cooperate with us."

Forcing a shrug, Jay said, "We'll give him some time. I think he'll call. Or she will." His money was on the woman. Shelly would want to learn as much as she could to help her lover. He'd seen the way she looked at John Smith. Jay had also seen the way John looked at her.

As if she were the center of his world.

Now Jay cleared his throat. "Look, it's the holidays. We made contact, the guy doesn't *seem* to be a threat. I can keep some security team members in the area to keep an eye on him, but it *is* almost Christmas. I know you want to be with Elizabeth. She wants to be with you."

"And you want to be with Willow."

Okay, that had just been hitting below the belt. Jay's eyes turned to slits. "It's not like that."

"Right." Sawyer gave him a hard smile. "Because she's your bait in the game we're playing."

It wasn't a game. There was one hell of a lot at stake. They were hunting Lazarus subjects, trying to see who was sane and who was a freaking wild killer, and they also had to stop the man who'd made the monsters in the first place.

Wyman Wright. The man who'd secretly been pulling strings to control the U.S. government for years.

Wright had taken Elizabeth's formula. And tried to make his own army.

"He knew Willow. I saw John Smith's reaction to her name."

Jay clamped his lips shut. He'd seen the guy's reaction, too. And he hadn't needed any hyper senses to do it. "They were in the same lab." He'd already known that Willow had been kept in a remote, North Carolina lab. He just hadn't realized that John Smith had been there, too.

"And there could be more subjects who were in that place, too," Sawyer added.

Willow hadn't remembered other test subjects.

But then, Willow had remembered very little.

"*That's* why we can't leave him with a surveillance team." Grim determination marked Sawyer's face. "The guy could give them the slip in a moment's time. We need to watch him. We need to convince John to join with us."

Jay could only shake his head. "And Elizabeth is going along with this? With you not being at her side for the holiday?"

"Elizabeth *will* be with me." Sawyer rolled back his shoulders. "We'll be using that private jet of yours, and she can come up here." His shoulder brushed against Jay's arm as he made his way to the door. "The town's fucking picturesque. She'll love it."

"Picturesque?" Jay followed him out of the apartment. "Dude, a guy was just killed here last night. We really need to talk about what picturesque means to you."

Jay had never liked small towns. To him, small towns hid the biggest secrets. And, sometimes, the worst monsters.

But he made his way down the stairs and to the bar. Jay shoved a twenty to the grizzled bartender. "Gonna be a long night," Jay muttered. "Give me something good."

The sheriff had been on the barstool to the right. But at his words, the guy got up and marched out, not even looking back.

Jay saluted the fellow with the glass he'd just been given. There he went, making friends left and right.

Truly the story of Jay's life.

CHAPTER FOURTEEN

"I think it looks good." Shelly smiled as she took a step back to admire her work. She'd covered all of the Christmas tree's bald spots with ornaments, and she'd layered up the lights. "Just needs a star." She turned, offering the golden star to John. "Want to do the honors?"

He stared down at the star in her hand as if he had absolutely no clue what he was supposed to do with it.

"John?" Shelly prompted softly. "Will you put the star on top?"

He swallowed. She saw his Adam's apple bob. He'd helped her with the decorations, hanging them all ever so carefully, as if they were made of diamonds and not just gleaming, gold balls made of plastic.

"Maybe you should do it." He hadn't taken the star. "Seems important."

A laugh slipped from Shelly. "The star *is* the most important part, but I want you to put it on the tree." She winked at him, wanting to push away the tension that cloaked him. "Besides, you're a lot taller than I am. That means you're good for the job."

He took the star, his fingers brushing against hers. As she watched, he reached up and put the star on the top. The star immediately began to slide to the left as it bent the branch, but John grabbed it, straightening the star—and its branch—quickly.

"Perfect," Shelly announced as she backed up a bit more and stared not at the tree, but at him.

Only John didn't see her gaze. He was busy staring at the tree. She'd hoped the tree would make him happy, but his features were still tense and far too guarded.

She knew why.

The men they'd met in town. The stories about test subjects being *wrong*.

She had to show John that there was nothing wrong with him. That *he* was absolutely perfect.

"What next?" John glanced her way. "Are you tired? Do you want—"

"You," Shelly finished.

He blinked.

She let her smile widen. *I'll show him. He'll believe me.* "I said we'd make new memories, and that's what we're doing. New memories and new traditions."

"I don't understand."

She glanced down at the rug that lay in front of the fireplace. "I think that we should do this every year. Put up our tree, and then make love by the fire."

"*Shelly…*"

"Until we have kids," she added, thinking this through. "Because then we'll have to change things up a bit. We'll put up the tree, and then after the kids go to sleep, we'll—"

He grabbed her, lifting her into his arms and bringing them eye to eye. "You…can't."

"I can't what?"

"You can't want kids with me." His words were so guttural. So painful to hear. And his eyes blazed with pain.

She wanted to take all of his pain away. So she kept a soft smile on her face and said, "I can want that. Not today. Not tomorrow. Because I want time with you. Just us. Time for us to get to know each other. Time to make more memories." His hold tightened on her. "But one day, yes, I do want kids. And I think you'd be an incredible father."

"What if I'm—"

"*Don't.*" Her smile was gone. She pulled out of his arms, making him put her back on the floor. "Don't say you're wrong. Because you're not. The man I'm falling in love with—he *isn't* wrong. He's good and he's strong, and I can count on him to never let me down. So don't you dare say anything negative about him."

His face had gone slack with shock. "You're...you think you could love me?"

Oh, John. I think I already do. "I know I could." Then she was grabbing his shoulders, pulling him toward her, pushing her mouth against his. Kissing him with all of the need and desire she felt. Showing him how much she wanted him. How much she cared.

They slid down to the rug. Pulled off each other's clothes. Kissed. Stroked. Laughed. Because this time, she just felt happy with him, and he finally seemed happy, too. Like her words had unlocked something inside of him.

Her hands went to his cock. His heavy, thick cock, and she leaned down to press a kiss to the head. John's breath rushed out and his laughter died. "No, baby, if you do that..."

She just pushed him onto his back. She slid over his body, and she tasted him in front of the fire. With the Christmas lights shining on them, with the scent of fresh pine filling the air, she savored him. Showed him how much she cared.

But he took over, rolling her beneath him. John caged her beneath him on the rug, and when he stared down at her, his expression was so fierce.

His cock shoved at the entrance to her body, but he didn't sink into her, not yet.

"Every Christmas," John gritted out, "just like this?"

She swallowed. "Every one."

He drove into her. Her back arched because he felt so good. So incredibly good. Her legs wrapped around him as he thrust, sliding in and out.

"Best…tradition…ever…" John's deep voice rumbled.

Her nails raked down his back. The heels of her feet dug into his ass. His hand slid between them, stroked her clit, sent her careening right into her orgasm.

She gave a little scream as she came. His cock shoved deep into her once more, sliding over her clit and sending a wave of pleasure spiraling through her again.

"I love you," he whispered, and then he was coming. She felt the burst of his release inside of her. Hot. Sexy.

Her heart thundered in her chest. So incredibly fast. She couldn't quite catch her breath, and Shelly didn't even care. John was on top of her, still *in* her, and she decided he was absolutely right. "Best…ever…" Shelly panted.

He laughed, and the sound warmed every single inch of her. She looked up and saw the star on the tree top.

A new memory had just been made.

***

"Someone's coming." John tensed when he heard the distant sound of the engine. He was in bed with Shelly, his body wrapped around her, and he'd planned to thrust *in* her again but...

Someone was coming to the cabin. It was after midnight. No one should be on that stretch of private road.

"What?" Her voice was drowsy. Sexy as all hell. She lifted her head, sending her hair trailing over the pillow. "Are you sure?"

Absolutely. "We need to get dressed."

And they dressed in silence. His body was tense, adrenaline already pumping through him. The threats to Shelly should be gone. They should be safe.

"Do you think it's the men we met in town?" Shelly asked, her expression turning thoughtful. "Sawyer and Jay? Are they trying to talk to you again?"

He hesitated and then...He gave a psychic push. *Sawyer, that had damn well better not be you coming to my mountain.* He used the same path that Sawyer had created in his mind earlier, and sending that message seemed as easy as breathing.

What in the hell are you talking about? Sawyer's instant response. As clear as if the guy had just spoken from right beside him. *I lingered a while at Sammy's bar. Talked to the owner, a real character who seems to know your lady pretty well.*

Sawyer could be lying but...

It didn't feel like a lie.

And then the car was closer. He recognized the sound of that particular engine. *Fuck. It's the sheriff.* Why the hell would Blane be there at that time of night?

Is something wrong? Now worry came clearly from Sawyer. *I know where the cabin is. Actually, I'm not too far away. Jay and I can be there —*

But John cut the link in his head. "It's the sheriff," he said to Shelly. "And he's coming in fast."

They dashed downstairs. He glanced outside the front window, watching as the sheriff brought his car to a fast halt. The sheriff rushed out of the vehicle and headed straight for the cabin. "He's alone," John added, frowning.

"Why didn't he just call?" Shelly's fingers slid over his back.

Something was wrong. Very wrong.

John unlocked the front door, letting in a blast of cold air and snow. "Blane." He motioned for the guy to come inside. Blane's heartbeat was racing and the fellow was sweating like mad. The faint scent of alcohol clung to him. "What's going on?"

Blane slammed the door shut behind him. Locked it. His fingers were shaking. "Those bastards in town. They're grilling Sammy.

Talking to everyone. Trying to learn as much as they can about you both."

Shelly hurried toward him. "You don't trust them."

"Hell, no. I don't. I don't *know* them." Blane's fingers slid toward his gun, moving nervously. "After everything that's happened lately, do you blame me?"

No, John didn't blame him.

"Shouldn't have gotten that last drink," Blane mumbled. "Shelly, shit, I hate to ask, but do you have any coffee? I know it's helluva late, but we've got to talk. There are things going on that you don't understand."

"I'll put some coffee on." She nodded briskly. "Go into the den, I'll be right back."

John turned, heading for the den. He could feel Blane behind him.

Shelly was hurrying for the kitchen, her steps light, but she paused and turned back around. "Blane, do you like straight black — *Blane!*"

John spun around, too. Blane had yanked out his gun. He was aiming it straight at John's head.

"Shot to the head and you don't come back," Blane snarled. "*You don't come back.*"

John leapt for the guy.

"That's what Jay said, shot to the —"

John hit him. But Blane had already fired and the bullet exploded from the gun.

CHAPTER FIFTEEN

The thunder of the gun was too loud. The men crashed to the floor as Shelly rushed toward them.

Bam. Bam.

Two more shots.

And…

John was on the floor. Not moving. There was blood streaming from his temple.

Blane staggered to his feet. His hand was shaking as he took aim again. "Let's be real sure that you *don't* come back again, asshole."

Shelly threw her body at him. They collided with a force hard enough to make her bones shudder before they slammed into the little table nearby. It splintered beneath them, sending a lamp shattering to the floor. She rolled fast and surged to her feet, aware of blood spilling from her wrist where a thick, glass shard of the broken lamp had lodged. The shard was long and jagged, and it hurt like a bitch. "*Stop!*"

He still had the gun. The bastard hadn't dropped it, but at least he hadn't been able to shoot John again. And her body was between Blane and John now.

"I won't let you do it," Shelly swore. "You'll have to kill me before you can get to him."

But Blane...laughed. Laughed as he holstered his weapon. "Oh, Shelly, that was always the plan."

She shook her head.

He bent and pulled a knife out of his boot.

Fumbling, she yanked the chunk of glass out of her wrist. More blood flowed, but she ignored the wrenching pain. She wanted to look back at John, to see if he was still alive, but she didn't dare take her gaze off Blane.

"Can't kill you with my service weapon." Blane gave a little shrug. "That wouldn't make sense." His gloved fingers gripped the knife. "So I'll use this, and then I'll put it in John's hand. My bullets are in him because, well, someone had to save the day after he attacked *you*, and, of course, I was just the man for the job."

"Your plan is a whole freaking lot like Devin's was!"

He smiled at her. Took a step toward her. She instantly slid back.

"It is," Blane agreed. "Because we were working together. It was all supposed to be so easy." His gaze darted over her shoulder. "Who the fuck knew a *super* soldier was going to come to your rescue?"

Her bloody fingers curled around the chunk of glass. She used her right hand because she could barely feel the fingers of her left. She didn't want to look at her wound to see how bad it was. "You were working with Devin."

"I just said I was, didn't I? I mean, shit, what did you expect me to do?"

"I don't understand. We were friends—"

"You and your brother had the company. You had all the money. God, Shelly!" A sharp bark of laughter came from him. "You didn't even *care* about the company! You spent your days painting pictures and not even noticing the world around you! I thought at first that I could romance you, get you to marry me, and then I'd take what was mine. I mean, I always kind of liked you. But you screwed that up, didn't you? Backed away from me before I had any real chance."

"We were friends," Shelly said again. She was talking mostly to buy herself time. To buy John time. She kept telling herself that he just needed time to heal. But Jay's voice replayed in her head. *I'll make sure that you stay permanently dead. A bullet to the brain will do that to your kind.*

"You know who else was *friends?*" Blane demanded, tossing her word back at her. "My dad and your father. They were such fucking good friends that they worked together up here in the mountains, they invented together, but your asshole of a father stole the ideas my old man created. He took the inventions. He patented them. He got all the money, and I got left with jackshit."

Her heart surged in her chest. "That isn't true."

"It fucking is!" Blane screamed. "My dad didn't think the shit they made was going to be worth anything. Thought they were just tinkering around. He signed the rights away. Let your dad pay him five grand for them. Five freaking grand! Then your dad walked away and made millions."

Her breath came faster. Harder.

"My dad died when I was eighteen. I'd just found the papers he signed. I *knew* he'd helped to build that damn company. Your dad came to me. You know what he did?" Blane didn't give her a chance to respond before he blasted, "Offered to pay for my fucking college. Like that was going to make us even. I asked him about my dad's inventions. And your father *lied* to my face. He said the things he'd done with my father hadn't helped the company. That he'd had to completely change them, redevelop them. Bullshit!"

"Blane—"

"I wanted what was mine. Even after your dad died, I had to stay on this godforsaken mountain, waiting, watching, as Charles got more and more money."

And the rage inside of him had grown.

"Then Charles took a partner." More laughter spilled from him. "But it wasn't long before good old Charles found out that Devin had been taking money from the company." Blane's lips curled in a humorless smile. "I heard them arguing one day, outside of Sammy's. Charles was going to fire Devin. Going to cut the man off without anything. And I saw my opening."

Her gaze dropped to the knife in his hand. She had a flash of facing Devin again. For an instant, she could see his face so clearly. She'd accused him of killing her brother. His eyes had gleamed and instead of a confession, he'd just said, "*Did I?*"

Pain twisted in her stomach. "There were no signs of a forced entry at my brother's house. The police thought he knew his attacker. That he let the guy inside. He didn't even fight back because he didn't see the attack coming."

Blane glanced at the knife in his hand.

Shelly swallowed. Blood kept dripping onto the floor near her as her wrist bled and bled. "Devin didn't kill my brother, did he?"

"Devin was supposed to take out the bodyguard your brother had tailing you." Anger roughened Blane's voice. "Turns out that asshole was harder to kill than we thought."

Her shoulders stiffened, her spine straightened, and an ice-cold rage filled every vein in her body as she tightly gripped the chunk of glass. "You killed my brother."

"I was just taking back what was *mine.* Years I spent up here, watching him get richer and richer and—"

She flew at him. Ran straight for him and slashed him with the chunk of glass. He wasn't prepared for her attack. The jerk had still been going on and on about how he *deserved* his cut of the money. She sliced him across the face, cutting into his cheek. He yelled and instinctively lifted his hand to shield his face. People always cared so much about their faces. He was so busy defending himself that he wasn't striking back.

She sliced again, cutting across the arm he'd raised. Then she drove the chunk of glass at his stomach, shoving it as hard as she could.

He stumbled back.

"My brother worked for everything he had! So did my father." Her breath heaved out. "I *saw* your dad's old designs years ago, you dumbass. They didn't work. They never worked. Only no one said anything to you because we didn't want to tarnish your memory of your dad. My father gave him that five grand because your dad was broke, and he needed a loan from a friend. There was never any partnership—"

His hand closed around her throat. His left hand grabbed her throat and his right brought the knife up to her face. He put the blade right on her cheek. "You fucking bitch." He squeezed her neck harder, choking her, and she could only gasp. Spittle flew into her face as he demanded, "Did you think a chunk of glass was going to stop me?" His breath blew over, and the scent of alcohol was so strong. He'd gotten his liquid courage, then he'd come up there to kill her.

She thought he'd slice open her cheek. But he didn't.

He laughed at her again. "Glad you gave me a few wounds," he muttered. "It'll make my story more believable." He stopped choking her but moved the knife down to her throat. "Got anything you want to say?"

Not to him. "I love you, John."

Blane's eyes widened. "What the fuck—"

"*Sweetheart, I love you, too.*"

Blane hauled her forward. Twisted her around so that her back was against his chest and his arms looped around her. He kept the knife at her throat, cutting into her skin so that blood spilled from her neck. Not deep enough to kill, but the threat was there.

And she saw John. Standing near their Christmas tree. Blood dripped down his temple, covering the side of his face. His shirt was wet with blood, too, as if he'd been shot in the chest, and she remembered hearing the extra blasts of gunfire.

"No!" Blane screamed. "I shot you in the head! I heard what that bastard said in town — a shot to the head will kill you! I shot you —"

"Shelly's scream warned me. I was able to dodge a direct hit." John's smile was absolutely terrifying because it promised death. "You grazed my head. The bullet didn't go into my brain." He waved toward his chest. "These wounds took me out for a bit, but as you can see, I'm back now." He pointed at Blane. "And you're a dead man."

Shelly was smiling. She couldn't help it. A knife was at her throat, but John was back. She'd bought him the time he needed. Blane wasn't going to win.

"Stay away from me!" Blane blasted. "Or I will slice her from ear to fucking ear! She'll be dead before you can reach me."

Was it true? Or was John faster? She could see the struggle on his face. He wanted to lunge forward, but...

Blane pressed harder on her throat. She didn't make a sound, she wouldn't give Blane the satisfaction of making her cry out, but Shelly felt more blood slide down her neck as the pain deepened.

"Why won't you just *die*?" Blane's voice was shaking. So was the hand that held the knife as it cut across her skin. "Shit, I was so afraid that you'd remember me. I met you before. Charles introduced us the same day I killed the bastard. He'd hired you to watch Shelly, but I swear, you'd fucking gotten some kind of crush on her. You were telling Charles that you wanted to meet her, that you wanted to explain who you were. You thought you were going to have some kind of chance with her, and that would have screwed up *everything*. So I had to act. I took out Charles. Devin went after you, and then Shelly…"

Her right arm lifted, moving slowly.

"Devin wanted to kill you right away, but I thought maybe I'd try my old idea of marrying you, Shelly. I mean, too many deaths would have looked suspicious. No one could connect John and Charles, but both you and Charles? Siblings dead within such a short period? That would have been too much, too soon. So I had to bide my time. I knew you'd come up here for the holidays. You always do. That was going to be my chance."

"You…sabotaged my car, that first night…"

"No, that was Devin." He laughed. "I sabotaged *my own* car because I knew no one would ever suspect me then."

She hadn't suspected him. Shelly felt his mouth against her ear as he said, "You were either going to fall for me, or you were going to die."

"She's *not* dying," John snapped.

No, she wasn't planning to die. Shelly had too much that she wanted to do in this world. Moving as fast as she could, not stopping to worry about what might happen next, she drove her right elbow back into Blane's stomach, knowing she'd be hitting the same area she'd wounded earlier.

He let out a howl of pain, and she surged forward as his hold loosened, just for a moment, thinking this was her chance.

But Blane grabbed her. Caught her arm and nearly dislocated her shoulder as he spun her back toward him. He brought up the knife, drove it down at her—

"She's not dying." John's words. Only this time, they were said right next to her. Because he was there. He surged in front of her and the knife hit him. It sliced over his chest, but he just drove out his fist, slamming it into Blane's jaw.

Blane staggered back. The knife flew from his fingers. He scrambled, trying to get his gun.

But John was on him. John jerked the fellow to his feet, and John had Blane's gun in his hand before the sheriff could even make another sound.

John pointed the gun right at Blane's chest.
Blane stilled.

Shelly's right hand was at her throat, trying to stop the blood that kept sliding down her skin.

Her left hand hung limply at her side. She didn't feel the pain from that wrist any longer.

"Do it," Blane challenged John. "Pull that trigger. Let Shelly see you kill *again*. Let her see, let her know what she's going to be sleeping with for the rest of her life."

She knew exactly what John was and that BS crap Blane was spilling would never change her opinion of him.

John didn't pull the trigger. He glared at Blane.

Blane started to laugh. "I'm going to tell the world. Tell them what a freak you are. You're going to get hauled back to that lab. Be trapped there, kept as a prisoner—"

"No," Shelly's voice was quiet and clear. "You're the one who will be a prisoner. You're going to be locked up. Put away for the rest of your life." She lurched toward John, feeling a wave of dizziness wash over her. "And if you try to spread stories about him, who do you think will believe you? After all, no one can come back from the dead."

Rage twisted Blane's face. Such stark fury. "It should have been *mine!* The company, the money—all mine!"

"Don't worry, Sheriff," John told him coldly. "I'm sure you'll get *exactly* what you have coming to you." Then John drove his fist into Blane's face again, knocking the guy out. Blane crumpled to the floor.

It only took John seconds to cuff him, using the handcuffs that had been on Blane's belt. John secured the cuffs tightly in front of Blane's body. And then John was reaching for Shelly. Pulling her into his arms. Holding her tight.

As tightly as she held him.

"God, baby," John whispered. "That knife at your throat…" And he pulled back, his hands moving to gently touch her skin. "Shit, we need to get you to town. You're going to need stitches."

"I-I meant what I said."

A furrow appeared between his brows.

"I love you," Shelly told him.

His face softened. His eyes gleamed. John pressed a soft kiss to her mouth. So tender.

"We're getting you to town," he whispered against her mouth. "Then after you're patched up, I'm taking you to bed. And keeping you in my arms until Christmas is over."

Sounded good to her. She swallowed and forced her lips to curl. Her stomach was twisting and dizziness slid through her again as the adrenaline started to crash, but she didn't want him to think she was weak so Shelly just stiffened her spine.

John grabbed Blane and started hauling him back outside. With her right hand, Shelly scooped up the gun that had been left behind, and she followed him out. John dumped Blane into the back of the sheriff's cruiser. John left the back door open as he glared at the unconscious man.

As she stood on her porch, Shelly saw the bright glare of headlights coming her way. She frowned into the glare, but John didn't seem worried. He turned toward the approaching vehicle, putting his hands on his hips.

The vehicle's doors opened. Sawyer Cage and Jay Maverick jumped out.

"We got here as fast as we could!" Jay called. "Good thing we were near this way when Sawyer got your distress signal—"

"Behind you!" Sawyer bellowed.

Shelly's gaze flew to John. No, *behind* John. Blane had jumped from the back of that cruiser. He held a gun in his still cuffed hands.

Back-up weapon. The bastard had a back-up weapon hidden on him.

Blane was aiming that weapon at John. At his head.

No! Shelly had a shot. She took it. The bullet blasted from the gun she held, and it found its target.

Blane's mouth gaped open. His eyes whipped to her. He fell, collapsing in the snow, and the white soon turned to red beneath him.

Sawyer and Jay ran toward Blane's collapsed form, but John—John hurried to Shelly's side. She was still aiming the gun.

"Baby..." His voice was hoarse.

The light-headedness she felt got worse. Just how much blood had she lost? Shelly glanced down at her left wrist. Blood soaked her hand. And the porch beneath her was covered with a pool of her blood.

"I think...I do need those stitches..." Her body swayed.

John scooped her into his arms. "Shelly?"

Her eyes started to sag closed. She'd stopped Blane. John was safe. And she...

"Love you," Shelly whispered, and she felt John's arms tighten around her. He'd take care of her, she knew it. Things would be okay.

After all, they had to be. This was Christmas. She and John were just starting their new traditions.

Everything *had* to be okay.

CHAPTER SIXTEEN

"It's hard when you love someone, and you're like we are."

John turned at the low words, and he found Sawyer Cage staring at him. He was in the hospital waiting room. Shelly was being stitched up. Sonofabitch—why hadn't he realized just how much blood she was losing? Her left wrist had been badly cut. She'd literally been bleeding out, and he hadn't even noticed.

She'd saved his life. She was his life. *And I didn't notice.*

"We're not quite human, any longer," Sawyer continued, seeming to carefully choose his words. "And we think we can change everything out in the world. That we should be strong enough to always protect those we care about."

John's hands had clenched into fists. He paced in the narrow waiting room as snow fell outside. "I failed her."

"She's going to be okay. Jay bribed one of the nurses—Shelly is already being transferred to a room. Your lady will pull through just fine. They gave her some transfusions, stitched her up. She's all right, I assure you."

John immediately bounded toward the double doors, but Sawyer stepped into his path. John's eyes narrowed. "Get the fuck out of my way."

Sawyer just inclined his head and didn't move the fuck out of John's way. "You're luckier than most. You have memories of her. And that's good. You're connected to her. You're grounded. You have humanity because of her."

He didn't know what the hell the guy was going on about—

"I don't have to worry," Sawyer continued grimly, "that you'll lose control. That you'll give in to the darker impulses that thrive inside of the test subjects."

Now John's attention sharpened. "Sonofabitch. You came to Discovery because you thought you were going to have to kill me."

Sawyer shrugged. "Kill…contain. Threat assessment was my number one priority. But you—you're not a threat. You're a man in love. A man who will do anything for the woman he wants." He clapped a hand on John's shoulder. "You're a lucky bastard."

"No, *you* are. Because if you'd tried to kill me…" John bared his teeth in a cold smile. "Guess which one of us would have hit the ground first?"

But Sawyer just laughed. "I swear, I think we're going to be good friends, man. And it's nice to have someone else on the team."

He hadn't joined any team.

Had he?

Sawyer squeezed his shoulder. "Enjoy Christmas with your angel. I'll spend my holiday with mine. And then we'll talk. I truly think we can help each other."

***

Shelly opened her eyes. A white ceiling was above her head, and the bitter scent of antiseptic stung her nose.

A hard, strong hand squeezed hers. "It's all right. You're safe."

Her head turned. She stared at the man beside her. The wrong man. "What in the hell are you doing here?"

Jay flashed her a broad grin. "Not the fellow you thought to find at your bedside? What? I can care. I can be a good person."

She snatched her right hand from his. "Where is John?"

"I suspect he is currently rushing down the hallway to find you. I got the jump on him because I had plenty of cash to bribe the nurses." His grin vanished. "And since we both know how fast a super soldier can be, let's just cut to the chase."

Her heart seemed to lurch in her chest. "What do you want?"

"I want you to work your considerable charm on your lover. The guy would literally do anything for you, that's obvious to anyone. Get him to see reason. Sawyer and I don't want to hurt him. We want to help John."

She actually did believe that.

"I want him to help me with Willow."

The name had her tensing. And when she tensed, the machines around her began to beep way too fast.

Jay exhaled and glanced toward the door. "Willow is with me. She remembers nothing about her past. Unlike John, she didn't have a connection with anyone — nothing that can jump start her memories. So I'd really like for John to see her. To talk with her. To tell us everything he can about the facility in North Carolina."

"Why don't you just go to the facility? Search it for yourself."

"I would, but the place has been completely obliterated."

Once more, her heartbeat increased.

"Just get him to talk with her," Jay urged her as his gaze slid back to Shelly. "Get him to give us all a chance."

"I'm not making any promises."

"No, I don't suppose you will...because you'd do anything for him, too, wouldn't you?"

She didn't answer.

"Must be nice, having that kind of bond."

It was.

"I should get out of here," Jay muttered. "Don't really relish the idea of John taking a swing at me." He gave her a little nod. "I guess we'll be seeing each other. Or, at least, I hope we will." He headed for the door.

"Stop."

He did. Jay glanced back at her.

"I *will* talk to him because I think John deserves to know more about what happened."

Relief flashed on Jay's face.

"But I'm not making any promises. What John decides to do—that's his decision, and I'll support him."

"Fair enough."

She thought it was. "But I want something from you."

His brow furrowed.

"I know about you," Shelly added quickly. "Most of the world does. You don't get to be *Time's* man of the year without having people know some of your secrets."

"I was man of the year *twice*," he groused, looking a bit insulted.

She wouldn't like him. Or...maybe she would. "You can do anything with a computer. Find anything."

He shrugged one shoulder. "I do have my skills."

"Help me find out more about John's past. Give me pictures. Give me moments that would matter to him."

"Memories." Now he appeared uncertain. "I can't make memories—"

"Pictures, videos. Give me something that I can show him. It's not fair that he lost it all."

Jay's gaze turned distant. "Willow did. You think I didn't look for her past? I can't find a damn thing for her. It's as if she never existed." He cleared his throat. "I'll try, okay?" He reached for the door. "But like you said, no promises."

Then he was gone.

The small hospital room seemed far too quiet. Shelly peered at her left wrist—it was covered in thick bandages. She still felt weak as all hell, and she noticed that an IV was feeding into her arm. Her hand lifted and she touched her neck—or rather, the bandages over her neck. Fear snaked through her. Just how much blood had she lost?

The door swung open. "*Shelly.*"

John was there. Rushing toward her. The machines around her went absolutely crazy once more as she reached for him.

He practically climbed into bed with her. Wrapped her tight in his arms. Held her so close. She could feel his own heart racing against hers.

"Scared the hell out of me," John whispered. His mouth was near her ear. "Baby, please, leave the dying to me."

No. She pushed against him. His head lifted. He stared into her eyes. "No one is dying again." Shelly wanted to be clear on this point. "No one."

His eyes were so bright. "You killed for me."

Because she wasn't so sure she could have lived without him. "I thought it was time we tried something new. Me…guarding you."

John swallowed. "I love you so much."

Only fair, really, because she'd given her heart and soul to the soldier who'd found her on a snowy mountaintop.

He kissed her. Softly. Tenderly.

***

"It's Christmas."

John's eyes opened.

Shelly was perched in the bed beside him, her beautiful hair tousled, her eyes so deep and dark. A white bandage was still around her neck—and another, thicker one covered her wrist. She'd been released from the hospital on Christmas Eve. They'd gone back to the cabin. Sawyer and Jay had cleaned up the place, put everything back to normal before Shelly and John had arrived home.

Things won't ever be normal. But Shelly seemed okay with his very non-normal self. In fact, he could see the love on her face right then.

"It's time for presents." Her smile stretched. "Come on, hurry up, sleepyhead. Presents are waiting downstairs. Presents should *never* have to wait."

And she darted from the room.

He pulled on a pair of jogging pants and followed her down the stairs. There was no sign of the chaos that had happened before. Everything was back in place. Jay and his resources were definitely useful.

Shelly sat on the rug near the tree. She'd already started a fire. He hadn't even heard her when she'd been rushing around. A big, brightly wrapped package was cradled in her hands.

He stared at her a moment, lost.

"John?" Her smile slipped. "Is something wrong?" Then she bit her lip, and her gaze darted around the cabin. "We shouldn't have come back here. I just—I wanted so badly to make Christmas work, and I'm sorry—"

He knelt in front of her. "Nothing's wrong. You're here. Everything is exactly right."

Her smile came back, but it wasn't as bright as before. Silently, John cursed himself. He never wanted to dim Shelly's smile. Never.

"Open this first," she urged him. Her fingers were shaking a bit as she handed him the package.

He'd wanted her to open a gift first. John hesitated. "Baby…"

"Please? It's important."

He'd never be able to refuse her anything. He opened the package, not tearing the paper but instead slowly pulling it away. Shelly had wrapped it, and he wanted to use care.

She laughed. "John, you're supposed to rip a package open because you're excited."

He was staring at a white box. He opened the box and found photographs inside. Photos of a boy riding a red bike. Photos of the same boy standing in front of a Christmas tree, grinning as he looked up at a pretty blonde woman. The boy and the woman were both wearing reindeer antlers. As he stared at that photo, his chest seemed to grow heavy.

"That's your mom," Shelly said quickly. "There are photos of your dad, too. And a dog you had when you were a kid and—"

"How?" His voice was shaking.

"I asked Jay to look for them. The guy can locate just about anything. I mean, he tracked you, after all. And I was sure there had to be pictures of your life out there."

He was staring at his mother. And in that picture, his mother was gazing down at the little boy — *at me* — with so much love on her face.

"You had a life, John. It was a good life. You were a good man." Shelly leaned forward and pressed a kiss to his cheek. "And you're going to go on and keep living a good life."

He had to blink, fast, and then he focused on her. Carefully, ever so carefully, he put the photos down. He knew he'd look at them a thousand times. Always. But first, there was something else he had to do.

John reached into the pocket of his jogging pants. He found the small box he'd slipped in there, the box he'd carefully hidden from Shelly. Before they'd returned to the cabin, he'd snuck away to make a purchase. Jay had wired some of John's funds to him, and he'd made quick work of finding Shelly what he hoped would be the perfect gift.

"John?"

He was kneeling in front of her. The lights from the tree and from the fire flickered over her, and he'd never seen anything more beautiful. He offered his small gift to her.

She ripped it open. Tore the wrapping paper away in a blink. And saw the black box that waited for her. So much smaller than the box she'd given to him.

Shelly opened the box. The diamond inside gleamed.

"I love you," John told her. *She* was the best gift he'd ever gotten. And he'd treasure her always.

A tear slid down her cheek. Shelly put the ring on her finger. Stared at it. Then at him.

"Shelly…" John cleared his throat. "I know it's soon but…do you think…would you ever want…" His words trailed away. *Would you ever want a life with me?*

"I love you, John," Shelly replied softly, but with certainty. "And it's soon, and I don't care. I want *you*." She threw her arms around him. They tumbled back onto the rug.

She kissed him. He kissed her. They laughed.

The darkness inside of him…it was quiet. Still.

Because he was happy. So happy.

He'd found her.

And she'd saved him.

The End

A NOTE FROM THE AUTHOR

Thanks so much for reading STAY WITH ME! I love Christmas, and I couldn't wait to write a book that would allow me to set my "Lazarus Rising" world during the holiday season. I wanted my characters to enjoy the season, but, of course, they had to survive danger and deception first. My favorite scene in the book was actually Shelly and John's Christmas tree buying moment. Despite the madness around them, they were taking some time to find a bit of joy. I hope you can find joy during this busy time of the year, too.

If you haven't read the other "Lazarus Rising" books, be sure to check out the first book in the series, NEVER LET GO. All of the books can be read as stand-alone stories, but I think it's more fun to read the full series.

Happy Holidays!

If you'd like to stay updated on my releases and sales, please join my newsletter list.

http://www.cynthiaeden.com/newsletter/

You can also check out my Facebook page. I love to post giveaways over at Facebook!

http://www.facebook.com/cynthiaedenfanpage

Again, thank you for reading STAY WITH ME.

Best,
Cynthia Eden
www.cynthiaeden.com

ABOUT THE AUTHOR

Award-winning author Cynthia Eden writes dark tales of paranormal romance and romantic suspense. She is a New York Times, USA Today, Digital Book World, and IndieReader best-seller. Cynthia is also a three-time finalist for the RITA® award. Since she began writing full-time in 2005, Cynthia has written over eighty novels and novellas.

For More Information

- *www.cynthiaeden.com*
- *http://www.facebook.com/cynthiaedenfanpage*
- *http://www.twitter.com/cynthiaeden*

HER OTHER WORKS

Romantic Suspense
Lazarus Rising

- Never Let Go (Book One, Lazarus Rising)
- Keep Me Close (Book Two, Lazarus Rising)
- Stay With Me (Book Three, Lazarus Rising)
- Run To Me (Book Four, Lazarus Rising) – Coming in January of 2018

Dark Obsession Series

- Watch Me (Dark Obsession, Book 1)
- Want Me (Dark Obsession, Book 2)
- Need Me (Dark Obsession, Book 3)
- Beware Of Me (Dark Obsession, Book 4)
- Only For Me (Dark Obsession, Books 1 to 4)

Mine Series

- Mine To Take (Mine, Book 1)
- Mine To Keep (Mine, Book 2)
- Mine To Hold (Mine, Book 3)
- Mine To Crave (Mine, Book 4)
- Mine To Have (Mine, Book 5)
- Mine To Protect (Mine, Book 6)
- Mine Series Box Set Volume 1 (Mine, Books 1-3)
- Mine Series Box Set Volume 2 (Mine, Books 4-6)

Other Romantic Suspense

- First Taste of Darkness
- Sinful Secrets
- Until Death
- Christmas With A Spy

Paranormal Romance
Bad Things

- The Devil In Disguise (Bad Things, Book 1)
- On The Prowl (Bad Things, Book 2)
- Undead Or Alive (Bad Things, Book 3)
- Broken Angel (Bad Things, Book 4)
- Heart Of Stone (Bad Things, Book 5)
- Tempted By Fate (Bad Things, Book 6)
- Bad Things Volume One (Books 1 to 3)
- Bad Things Volume Two (Books 4 to 6)

- Bad Things Deluxe Box Set (Books 1 to 6)

Bite Series

- Forbidden Bite (Bite Book 1)
- Mating Bite (Bite Book 2)

Lazarus Rising

- Never Let Go (Book One, Lazarus Rising)
- Keep Me Close (Book Two, Lazarus Rising) - Available 10/24/2017

Blood and Moonlight Series

- Bite The Dust (Blood and Moonlight, Book 1)
- Better Off Undead (Blood and Moonlight, Book 2)
- Bitter Blood (Blood and Moonlight, Book 3)
- Blood and Moonlight (The Complete Series)

Purgatory Series

- The Wolf Within (Purgatory, Book 1)
- Marked By The Vampire (Purgatory, Book 2)
- Charming The Beast (Purgatory, Book 3)
- Deal with the Devil (Purgatory, Book 4)

- The Beasts Inside (Purgatory, Books 1 to 4)

Bound Series

- Bound By Blood (Bound Book 1)
- Bound In Darkness (Bound Book 2)
- Bound In Sin (Bound Book 3)
- Bound By The Night (Bound Book 4)
- Forever Bound (Bound, Books 1 to 4)
- Bound in Death (Bound Book 5)